IF
YOU
LIVED
HERE
YOU'D
ALREADY
BE
HOME

STORIES BY
JOHN JODZIO

SOFT SKULL

NEW YORK

Soft Skull Edition 2017

Library of Congress Cataloging-in-Publication Data Is Available.

Cover design by Kelly Winton
Book design by Sarah DeYoung

ISBN 978-1-59376-663-4

SOFT SKULL
New York, NY
www.softskull.com

Printed in the United States of America

The following stories were previously published in a slightly different form
in the following publications:

"The Bog Body," *Rake Magazine;* "Flight Path," *One Story;* "Mail
Game," *In Posse Review;* "Gravity," *Florida Review;* "Make-a-wish,"
Pindeldyboz, reprinted in *Big Ugly Review;* "The Dojo" and "Vessels,"
Pindeldyboz; "Monarchs" and "Shoo, Shoo," MNArtists; "Kalispell,"
Minnesota; "Inventory," *Bullfight Review;* "The Barnacle" and "If You
Lived Here, You'd Already Be Home," *Opium Magazine;* "Whiskers," *Five
Chapters;* "Alejandra," *Barrelhouse;* "Colonel Cheese," NatBrut; "Sleepy
Mom," Tin House Online; "Sugarfoot," Yemassee.

FOR KATE AND THEO

CONTENTS

COLONEL CHEESE IS
CLOSED ON MONDAYS

We lock the doors and pull our liquor from our purses and backpacks. Jake gets the whippets from the walk-in fridge. Cesar yells "Watch this!" and rips a Raleigh phone book in half. It's Sunday night. Colonel Cheese is closed on Mondays.

We're still in our work clothes, black button downs and red suspenders. There's pizza sauce ground into the carpet and the high chairs need to be uncrumbed. The singing robot bears up on stage are still hot to the touch. I pour tequila into a blue raspberry slushie and my assistant manager, Tom, hooks his arm through mine.

"Alexa," he says, "fifty bucks says you can't eat a pound of butter in two minutes."

I'm twenty-six. My ex-fiancée, Michael, called off our wedding six months ago. A few weeks later, fueled by grief, I won a nacho eating contest. Since then I've been hooked, spent my weekends traveling up and down the East Coast eating massive amounts of food as quickly as I can. Next weekend, I'll drive to Charlottesville to try to eat ten pounds of ham in ten minutes. After that I'll be in Vermont seeing how fast I can shovel two gallons of cottage cheese down my throat.

"I liked it better when you painted landscapes," my mom tells me. "I liked it better when you painted meandering rivers and limestone bluffs."

Last weekend I boxed up my oils and brushes and stuffed them into my storage space. For now, I'm done with nature; for now I'm done arching my hand carefully across a canvas to embellish a ripple in a creek or to make the evening sky ache with ochres and umbers.

"No one ever chanted my name when I painted landscapes," I tell my mom.

Tom slaps a fifty-dollar bill on the table. I waitress like a lot of other people waitress, to afford to do the thing I love which won't pay the bills. That used to be painting, but now it's hearing people cheer as I push potato skin after potato skin down my throat.

"Are you gonna puss out?" Tom asks.

Last week Tom bet me fifty bucks that I wouldn't take the garbage to the dumpster wearing only my bra and panties. The week before that, he bet me I wouldn't swallow one of the bottom feeders in the aquarium. I can't tell if Tom doesn't think I'll do these things or if they're just things he'll pay to see.

"Bring it on," I say.

Most of us at Colonel Cheese are newly single. Most of us are angry about that fact. Linda's boyfriend broke up with her because she tried to change him. Tom's wife left him because he's Tom. Jake's girlfriend caught him tonguing the back of Linda's knee in his pickup. I brought my wedding dress to work and set it on fire in the parking lot. The dress melted more than it burned; left a speed bump of white goo on the asphalt I drive over each day when I come to work.

Tom sets the butter down on the table and everyone gathers around. All of us wear nametags with fake names when we work. Right now I'm wearing a nametag that says Josie. Linda's nametag says Constance. Cesar's wearing a nametag that says Jason B. even though there is no other Jason's, fake or otherwise, who work with us.

"When you get bitched at with a name that's not your own the bitching doesn't stick," Linda told me when I first started.

I stare at the butter. It's only been out of the fridge for a minute, but it's already sweating.

"Go!" Tom yells.

I finish the butter in ninety seconds; slap my hands down on the table. Tom forks over the fifty. Everyone cheers.

"Time to dance!" Cesar yells.

Jake dims the lights, Tom cranks the sound system. Cesar grabs my hand to pull me onto the dancefloor, but I wave him off. A few Sundays ago, he tried to kiss me, but I slid my lips out of the way before he could.

"I'm not ready," I told him.

But now I decide I am. I stand up and shuffle my feet across the carpet, move slowly toward Cesar. I build up a bunch of static electricity in my body. When I get close I reach out my finger and touch it to Cesar's chest, watch it crackle with light.

SLEEPY MOM

My mom has narcolepsy so she bought a student driver car with a steering wheel in the passenger side seat. Whenever she drives anywhere, I ride shotgun. If she falls asleep while she's driving I'm supposed to elbow her awake. Sometimes I do and sometimes I don't. Sometimes when she nods off instead of hitting the brakes I press down on my gas pedal and drive over to the strip mall where my ex-girlfriend Sadie works.

Sadie just got her license, but I've got six months to go. Sadie works at Elaine's Boutique, a crappy jewelry store that sells shitty silver pendants and fake gold chains. No one goes to Elaine's so most days Sadie's new boyfriend, Eric, stops by to keep her company. Sometimes Sadie and Eric do their geometry homework, but mostly they snort Sadie's Ritalin and kiss long and hard like their tongues are a geometry problem they don't ever want to solve.

"Quit going there," my friend Jason keeps telling me. "Remove yourself from the equation."

I adjust the focus on my binoculars, watch Eric snake his hand up Sadie's shirt. My mom gently snores in the seat beside me, drool welling in the corner of her mouth.

"But that used to be me," I tell Jason.

My dad used to drive us everywhere, but he bolted three months ago. He sends us a letter every few weeks. His last letter said he was working on a fishing boat in Alaska. The postmark on the last letter was stamped "Cleveland," so we don't know what to believe.

"Cleveland or Alaska," my mom says. "The only thing that matters is he's gone."

This morning my mom and I drive to the grocery store. She makes it three blocks before her eyes slide shut. I drive the rest of the way. As I angle the car into a parking spot, Jason calls.

"Party at Clare Lowalke's tonight," he says. "Can you get the car?"

I look over at my mom, fast asleep, her face mashed against the driver's side window, her mouth wide open.

"No problem," I tell Jason.

I ask my mom if she wants to go to the Valley-Hi. It's a shithole drive-in outside town that's somehow hanging on.

"Wow," my mom says, "that would be lovely."

My mom takes a bath before we go. I stand outside the bathroom door listening to her sing. If she stops singing it means she's drowning. If she stops singing, I need to rush in and pull her out of the tub. She's only stopped singing in the bathtub once. I ran in and pulled her out of the tub right before her face slid under the water.

"We should do this kind of thing more often," she yells to me through the bathroom door. "We should make this a weekly thing."

"Absolutely we should," I say.

- - - - - - - -

On the way to the movie, my mom zonks out. I drive over to Jason's and pick him up.

"This is insane," he says. "What if she wakes up?"

"She won't," I tell him.

After I park the car I roll down the passenger side window for my mom. We walk inside Clare Lowalke's house, buy a cup for the keg. Everyone here is older than us, juniors and seniors, but they all know who I am.

"You're the kid with the sleepy mom, right?" one guy asks. "Does she smoke a lot of weed? Is that why she can't stay awake?"

I know Sadie's around here somewhere. I ditch Jason and wander around the party. I find her in one of the back bedrooms, passed out in Eric's arms. I wrote her another note explaining how special we were together and how special we could be again. When I set the note down next to her on the bed, her eyes snap open.

"What in the fuck?" she says, crumpling up the note and chucking it at me.

"I thought maybe we could talk things over again," I say. "I miss you."

"Maybe you'll understand this best," Sadie says, curling up in Eric's arms and closing her eyes.

After I drop Jason off, I poke my mom awake.

"You slept through the whole movie," I say.

"Why didn't you wake me up?" she asks.

"You looked so peaceful," I tell her. "You look like you needed the sleep."

I want to say something about Sadie, about how I'm going crazy over this breakup, but I don't. I keep my mouth shut, my hands at ten and two.

"How was the movie?" she asks.

"Really sad," I tell her.

The next day my mom and I take the car to get the oil changed. She falls asleep and I drive over to the strip mall one last time. While I'm sitting in the parking lot watching Sadie a young mother brings in her baby into Elaine's Boutique to get her ears pierced. The kid's maybe a year old, dressed in a pink frilly dress. I watch through my binoculars as Sadie props the baby up in the piercing chair. The baby's face is so damn happy, smiling and giggling, but then the piercing gun rifles through her ear and the baby's face is transformed into an angry red ball.

Sadie's a pro. While the baby screeches, she holds out a mirror in front of the baby's face. She whispers, shh, shh, look, look, little one, look how pretty. Soon the baby sees the jewels in her ears and the tears slide away. I find a sad song on the radio and I put the car in drive. I scream out the lyrics as I speed off. Now matter how loud I sing, my mom doesn't stir at all.

SUGARFOOT

A week after his stroke, Nelson took a crowbar to the padlock on the barn door. He found Corrine's Andalusian and slipped a bridle over the horse's head. He tucked himself against Sugarfoot's flank and they made their way down the red rock driveway and into the trailer attached to his idling pickup. By the time the sun rose, they were halfway across Kansas.

When Nelson stopped for gas outside Topeka, he left a voicemail with the woman from Camp Courage, telling her he had the horse for the sick kids that he'd promised. After the call, he took Sugarfoot out of the trailer and pranced him around —the horse had that strange, bouncing gait – it looked like he hated for his hooves to even touch the ground. They were a pair. Nelson's left leg dragged behind the rest of his body as he they circled around a blinking sign advertising fried chicken and cheap cigarettes.

Nelson was dying. Or he wasn't. No one could decide. The night doctor at Mercy said one thing; the day doctor the complete opposite. Back and forth, those jackasses, one telling Nelson to put his affairs in order, the other telling him that he'd live twenty years with certain dietary tweaks. Lab tests, scans of his head and heart, a week straight of being prodded and poked.

"How about now?" one of the nurses asked, pressing her thumb into his thigh. "Feel anything now?"

Nelson was sixty-two, too surly to be micro-managed, tired of wasting time fretting over the certainty of uncertainty. That last night in the hospital, when Corrine did not visit, Nelson yanked the wires from his chest and the IVs out of his arms and limped out of the hospital doors and down the white line of the county road all the way back home.

Nelson stole Sugarfoot out of spite. He stole the horse because he and Corrine had some good years living in a cabin in the shadows of the Tetons and then two months ago she'd come inside with a handful of cherry tomatoes curled in her blouse and told him she was leaving.

"Is there someone else?" he asked.

"Nope," she told him, dumping the tomatoes into a colander and turning on the faucet. "There's only us."

Corrine was ten years younger than him, skinny, still good-looking. Over the next week, Nelson stalked her. One afternoon he followed her Jeep to the Super Valu and watched her come out of the store with an ear of sweet corn and a can of soup. The next afternoon, he tailed her to the stables and watched her canter Sugarfoot over the show course.

One night, Nelson followed Corrine and her best friend Josie over to the Riverside Lounge. After three hours, the women skittered outside. Nelson slid lower in his seat, but Corrine noticed his truck and tromped over.

"I asked for space," she yelled. "It's a simple goddamn request."

"Space is bullshit," he snapped. "I never agreed to it."

"If you could see yourself right now," she said, "it wouldn't be such a mystery why I left."

After Corrine stormed off, Nelson drove home. He drank straight from a liter bottle of Don Rico and passed out on in the rotted wicker chair on his porch. When he woke up the next morning, he couldn't feel the left half of his body.

The next time Nelson and Sugarfoot stopped was outside Des Moines. Nelson took his hunting knife from his pocket and sliced up a Granny Smith, fed it to the horse with his good hand. He went inside the truck stop and paid for a shower. As he stood under the hot water he pressed his thumb into his thigh, over and over.

Nelson kept hoping there was something inside his body that simply needed to be reset, that one morning he would wake up and everything would be back to normal. He dried himself off and parted his hair. His new face was hard to grow accustomed to—one side of his mouth falling away, the other side set in a wincing grin.

While he ate his dinner, he paged through the brochure for Camp Courage. It was full of bald kids with ravenous eyes traversing the trials on their horses, able to forget their circumstances for a bit.

When Nelson finished his dinner, he walked out of the truck stop and saw the gate of the horse trailer swinging in the wind. Sugarfoot was gone. At first, Nelson thought he'd had another stroke, that he was hallucinating. He kicked around the bedding, knelt down and burrowed his hands into the straw, like that damn horse was hiding somewhere under there.

When he came out of the trailer, Nelson saw a woman standing on top of a dumpster. She was staring out the highway, her eyes tracking each car that sped past. The woman's bangs were cut straight across her forehead and her body was swimming in a thick wool sweater. There was a cigarette housed behind her left ear. She glanced at her watch and then refocused her gaze on the road.

"Someone stole the horse I stole," Nelson yelled up to her. "Can you believe that shit?"

As he walked closer, he could tell that this woman had been crying—her mascara tributaried down her cheeks and then disappeared down into the neck of her sweater.

"I heard some kids giggling a while back," she said, finally looking down at him. "Maybe there was a whinny in the middle of the laughter."

In the dim light, Nelson followed Sugarfoot's prance marks out of the trailer, but they disappeared when the ground turned to blacktop. He stared out toward a stand of trees in the distance as the woman climbed down off the dumpster and stood next to him. Her arms were thin and fingers bony. She placed one of her hands on Nelson's bad shoulder. He couldn't feel it, but that didn't mean he wasn't happy it was there.

"I'm Ellen," she told him. "And I'm thinking that it's best that I'm not alone right now, okay?"

Nelson huffed down a path worn through the switchgrass. Ellen thought the kids had taken Sugarfoot this way. Nelson fanned a flashlight in front of her feet like he was an usher guiding her down a darkened aisle.

"I ran inside to buy cigarettes," Ellen told him, "and then my fiancé Steve just drove off. No warning or nothing. When I get back to the gas pump, there's no car and no Steve. He did this to me one other time after we got in a fight. This time though, we were getting along just fine."

Ellen was downwind and Nelson could smell the scent her skin gave off —cocoa butter and sweated gin. It made him remember

Corrine, how she would come home after riding Sugarfoot and he would kiss her on the neck and taste sunblock under the dust.

"I kept telling Steve he was lucky to have me," Ellen said. "I thought that maybe if he heard it enough, he'd start to believe what I was saying."

They exited the stand of trees. Down the hill about a hundred yards away, Nelson saw Sugarfoot grazing. Ellen took off at a sprint. Nelson followed behind her as quick as he could.

By the time he caught up to Ellen, she was rubbing Sugarfoot's flank and whispering into his ear. Maybe she liked horses, Nelson thought. Maybe now that Steve had ditched her he'd try to sweet talk her into coming with him to Tennessee. Maybe she'd still be crazy or angry enough at Steve to say yes.

When Nelson got closer, he heard a rustling in the scrub. And then a man with shaved head and a goatee walked out, pointing a .45 at Nelson's chest.

"Hi there," the man said, giving a little wave to Nelson. "I'm Steve."

Steve was short and twitchy, wearing khaki shorts and flip flops. He wrapped his arms around Ellen and planted a hard kiss on her lips.

"I told you this would work," she said. "And he'll put up way less of a fuss down here, now won't he?"

Ellen had looked frail and pretty by the gas station, but now that she was grinning maniacally instead of crying, Nelson saw how shadowy and severe her face actually was, how his loneliness had blinded him to this fact.

"Toss over your wallet and the keys to the truck," Ellen told him.

Nelson pressed his left thigh with his thumb. Nothing. He looked over at Sugarfoot gnawing on some fescue a couple of yards away. He palmed the knife in his pocket.

"Am I supposed to ride the horse back home?" Nelson asked.

"Fuck if we care," Ellen said.

Nelson chucked his wallet and keys a few feet short of where they stood. For a second he thought about letting these dopes take what they wanted, letting them drive away without a fight, but now he had decided he wanted to make them earn their reward, show them how hard it was to take something from someone who had so little to lose. He guessed he had at least fifty pounds on Steve and so when that fucker knelt down to pick up the keys, Nelson charged.

Steve's first shot sailed wide. The second one nicked Nelson's stroked shoulder. Nelson leapt on Steve's chest, slapped the gun out of his hand. The two men wrestled in the high grass. Nelson reached for his knife, but Steve kicked himself free from Nelson's grip and scrambled to his feet. Ellen was sprinting up the hill already and Steve ran after her.

Nelson pressed his jacket against his wound. Stood up and coaxed Sugarfoot toward him. He was dizzy and his heartbeat filled his ears. When the horse came near Nelson draped his body over him like a saddle blanket and then urged the horse toward the lights of the gas station. Sugarfoot obeyed, strode forth, clomping his hooves up and down as he walked, tamping down the bitten undergrowth in the gully with each step.

THE EAR

Alexi's mother died and as was the custom in his family he sawed off her left ear. Before the police came, he slid the ear into a Ziploc bag and hid it amongst a box of turkey burgers in the freezer. When he led the officers upstairs to the body, he told them this was how he found her. Then he started to sob.

"Did she have any enemies?" one of the officers asked.

Alexi shook his head no. He'd just turned twenty three and his mother had been sick for the last year. Every night she made him practice his mourning face in the bathroom mirror. She taught him how to cry on demand by reminding him how his childhood dog, Shep, had been nailed by that mini-van.

"Remember all the dog blood squirting out of neck?" his mother asked. "Remember how the dog blood mixed with the snow and made the snow all pink?"

Even when Alexi cried perfectly, when he howled with real grief, his mother wasn't satisfied.

"The cops won't believe you're sad unless you make your eyes look like they're being sucked back into your skull," she told him.

As the cops moved around his house now, Alexi saw one of them pull a small flask from his pocket and take a quick gulp. Alexi could tell this cop was near his pension by the way he walked—one foot flat on the floor boards before the other foot even thought about leaving the ground. He put his hand on Alexi's shoulder, tried to calm him.

"I've long been resigned," he told Alexi, "to the backward thinkers of this world."

After his mother's funeral, Alexi's found his cousin Het standing outside the church. Alexi and Het had played together as kids, but Alexi hadn't seen him in years. He'd gotten occasional updates from his mother about him. He'd heard how Het had a metal plate in his head from a motorcycle crash, how he'd nearly died from a snake bite. Het gave Alexi a long, uncomfortable hug.

"You got the ear," Het said. "Good for you. My mom had a heart attack in a Long John Silver's bathroom. Way too many people around for me to get hers."

Alexi looked toward the street where a truck with a payload full of old appliances and scrap metal clattered past. In their family, this tradition was performed without fanfare, never discussed in public. Het knew this, had it drilled into him at any early age.

"Was it a big ear?" Het asked. "Like maybe big enough to share?"

Alexi looked up at the clouds, fingered his keychain. Het's button down shirt was baggy, the kind of shirt you might wear if the police had taped a microphone to your chest.

"Wonderful to see you, cousin," Alexi said, climbing into his car. "It's been far too long."

Three days after the funeral, Alexi went back to work. All of his co-workers at the bookstore had heard about his mother. Alexi was surprised to note that her death had brought out a kindness toward him that had been previously missing. He hadn't been well liked before, but now his co-workers offered him donuts, invited him along when they went to the Chinese buffet for lunch.

"Are there any clues?" his manager, Eric, asked. "Do the police have any leads?"

"Nothing," Alexi told him, "and they're not particularly hopeful."

There was a woman at work, Sophia, who began to take an increased interest in Alexi's welfare. She began to pick him up every morning for work. Most nights, she gave him a ride home. One night, instead of simply dropping him off, she got out of her car and followed him inside.

"We need to brighten things up around here," she said as she surveyed his living room. She was wearing a short skirt and a sweater that hung off her left shoulder. She ran her finger along a windowsill, held it up to show Alexi the dirt.

"I'm sorry," he told her. "I'm still grieving."

"Of course you are," she said, spinning open the living room blinds to let some light in. "I wouldn't have expected anything different."

Sophia went into the kitchen and filled up a coffee cup with water. She went around watering his mother's plants. After she was finished she sat down next to him. She took Alexi's hand in hers.

"Is this okay?" she asked as she nestled into his body.

"Sure," he said.

Soon she kissed his neck and then moved upward to his lips.

"My skirt unzips on the side," she whispered to him.

As was the custom, Alexi brewed tea with his mother's ear on the one month anniversary of her death. He wrapped the ear in cheesecloth just as his mother taught him. He steeped it in the traditional herbs and then poured the tea into the ceremonial cup with the family crest stamped on it. Drinking the tea would give him some of his mother's strength and wisdom. That was the idea anyway.

While he was sipping on the tea, Het knocked on his door. Alexi ducked under his kitchen table, hoping Het hadn't seen him.

"I'd recognize that ear tea smell anywhere!" Het yelled to him from outside. "Smells just like beef bullion."

At first Alexi thought Het might leave but after ten minutes straight of pounding on the door, Alexi let him in. Het knelt down in front of Alexi, holding up two crumpled twenties.

"For chrissakes," Alexi said, handing him the cup. "Put your fucking money away and take a fucking drink."

Sophia came over that night and Alexi made her spaghetti. He'd cleaned the apartment, dusted. After dinner, they sat down on the couch. He moved to kiss her, but she slid away.

"I think this relationship has run its course," she said.

"What?" he asked. "Why?"

"I only date sad men," Sophia said. "That's my thing."

She began to move around the house gathering up the things that she'd left there, a necklace, a book, her toothbrush.

Alexi made the face that his mother had taught him, thought about Shep and the mini-van and then tears poured from his eyes.

"Look," he told her. "I'm still horribly sad."

"That does look pretty sad," Sophia said, "but you might be faking."

Alexi buried his head in hands and sobbed uncontrollably. Soon he felt Sophia's arms around him and then they were pulling off each other's clothes.

Het showed up a couple of days later, looking worse than before.

"Nothing's changed," he said. "Nothing's improved. Maybe I needed more than a couple of sips of tea. Maybe I needed the entire cup."

"I've heard that sometimes it takes a while to work," Alexi told him, even though he'd never heard that from any of his relatives. "And I've heard that sometimes it doesn't work at all."

Het flopped down on the couch, closed his eyes, drifted off. Alexi couldn't summon the energy to make him leave, so he left him there, snoring. He called up Sophia.

"I'm totally sad now," he told her. "I can't stop crying. It seems like there isn't any point to any of this."

"You're probably leading me on," Sophia said, "but I like it."

"I'm thinking about taking some pills," he told her. "I'm thinking about cutting myself. I'm in a dark ass place."

"That sounds hot," she said. "I'll be right over."

Alexi dressed in all black and rubbed his eyes to make it look like he'd been sobbing. When Sophia arrived she didn't seem to notice his extra work because she was looking at Het sleeping on the couch.

"Who's that?" she asked.

"My cousin Het," Alexi said.

"He looks awful," she said.

Sophia and Alexi went into his bedroom, but Alexi could tell that she was distracted. They made out for a while and then Sophia told him she was exhausted and fell asleep. Alexi fell asleep next to her.

He woke around midnight and Sophia wasn't in bed. He got up and walked into the living room and he found her kissing Het.

"Shit," Het said, pulling away from her. "I'm sorry."

"I couldn't help it," Sophia told Alexi. "He's way sadder than you'll ever be."

Alexi ran into his bedroom and buried his head in his pillow and sobbed real tears. He thought that Sophia might come to comfort him, but instead he heard the two of them leave. They walked over to Sophia's car and drove away. Alexi got up and went to the kitchen. There was still a little bit of ear tea left in a Tupperware container in his fridge. He thought about dumping it down the sink but then he thought better of it and gulped the rest of it down.

WILLEM AND TRUDY, DEUCE AND ME

I was hired to care for Willem Cosgrove after his first hospice nurse quit. He was dying of lung cancer and between coughing fits he called out for someone named Doris. This was not his wife's name. His wife's name was Trudy. She was in the room next door. She was dying of bone cancer and luckily she could not hear for shit.

Trudy had her own home health care aid, Deuce. Sometimes Deuce brought a bottle of Captain Morgan and we sat at their kitchen table and drank. Deuce was married, but after Willem and Trudy were asleep, we'd usually make out or watch television.

"Lisa," Deuce told me once. "I'm totally falling for you."

Willem and Trudy were bedridden, but they still tried to talk to each other. Neither of them could hear and so Deuce and I were left to translate.

"Is he saying something about my fat arms?" Trudy asked. "He's always hated my arms."

"He says he loves you," Deuce said.

"Is she telling you I slept with her cousin?" Willem asked me. "That one's a lie."

"She says she misses your touch," I told Willem.

There was a bell by Willem's bedside that he rang when he needed me. Mostly what he wanted was water, but also he kept begging me to tickle him.

"C'mon," he said. "Just one time?"

"Maybe Trudy would like to tickle you," I said.

"Have you looked at her hands?" he said. "They're like garden tools. And don't even get me started on those fat arms of hers."

One night, when Trudy and Willem were asleep, Deuce and I ordered pizza. Then we got naked and rolled around their couch.

"This just feels right," Deuce said. "You know?"

I knew. I'd never looked forward to coming to work before, but now I hated to drive back to my lonely apartment with my stupid cat and my dumbass collection of state quarters that was still missing Oregon.

After a week of Willem begging me to tickle him, I gave in.

"Where?" I said.

He pointed to his armpit and I reached my hand under his nightshirt. Willem's face broke into a grin. He giggled a little, but then his face turned serious.

"Are you okay?" I asked.

"There comes a point when tickling turns into scratching," he said.

- - - - - - - -

Trudy died first. It was peaceful, in her sleep. The next day, Deuce was assigned to a new job across town.

"Can we still see each other?" I asked him.

There was a pause, a crackling across the phone line.

"Sometimes the loveliness of something is its utter convenience," he told me.

Willem died two days after Trudy, as often happens with couples who are deeply in love. I pressed his eyelids shut and called the ambulance.

"No need to hurry," I told the dispatcher. "He's not going anywhere."

After I made the call, I sat down next to Willem's bed. I took his hand and ran his fingers up and down my forearm, gently, lightly, over and over, until the paramedics arrived.

THE BOG BODY

Chucho and I were searching for golf balls in the protected wetland on the 12th hole when my feet found a body. There were already several hundred golf balls sitting on the edge of the marsh ready to be cleaned and sold and I'd dug my feet into the mud expecting to feel the cool dimpled cover of another one, but instead, I felt a face.

Buried in the mud, a golf ball feels like a rock, and you curl your foot like a hawk's claw and yank it out. Over the course of the summer, searching for golf balls in water hazards, my feet had become very sensitive. I likened them to a blind man's hands, something you could substitute for eyes.

Sometimes Chucho and I played this game where he dropped some pocket change on the sidewalk and I put my foot over it and told him exactly how much it was. It was useless knowing that there were seventy-eight cents underneath your foot instead of, say, eighty-two, but the skill came in handy at times like this. When I patted my toes around in the brackish water I knew right away that my foot was pressing down on someone's nose.

"There's a body buried where I'm standing," I told Chucho. I ran my big toe over its pursed lips. "And it didn't die happy."

"Hold still," Chucho told me.

He dove under the water to get a closer look. He was down there forever, swimming right by my feet. He came up with three golf balls, chucked them over to the shore.

"Well?" I asked.

"Bog body," he said. "I'll go get Dutty."

Dutty was the greenskeeper. He was a drunkard with a legendary mean streak, but he let us rummage around in the creeks and ponds on the municipal golf course in exchange for a cut on anything we sold. His mail-order bride had recently arrived, a Russian girl named Kika. Chucho and I figured it was partly our doing that Dutty had been able to finance such a venture. We were none too pleased.

Three days ago, instead of making us wait on the stoop when we dropped off his money, Dutty had ushered us inside.

"My trenchfooted friends," he'd said, "I'd like you to meet the missus."

His place smelled of grass seed and cigarette butts. There were bags of fertilizer leaning against his TV cabinet. Kika was sitting on the couch; she was smoking and watching a TV show about penguins.

"Boys, this is Kika," Dutty said. He turned to Kika. "Kika, these are the boys."

Kika glanced up at us for a second. She had dyed blond hair and a slightly turned-up nose. She grunted something in Russian and then returned to her TV show. She scratched her scalp and cracked her knuckles and then put her feet up on the milk crates that were doubling as a coffee table. She was sitting right there next to us, but I felt like we were staring at her in some sort of cage, waiting to see what she'd do next. She snuffed out her cigarette in an ashtray and immediately lit up another one.

Dutty extended his arm out beside Kika like he was showcasing a brand new coupe at a car show. He was beaming. I was thirteen, old enough to understand that I was expected to congratulate him.

"You're a lucky man," I said.

"I most certainly am," he crowed.

As I waited in the water for Chucho to return, I watched the endangered herons peck at their nests about thirty yards off, their urgent cawing and their skinny legs impatiently tamping the earth to find solid ground.

I didn't want to lose contact with the body, so I kept my right foot on its head while my left foot explored the rest. I could tell the body was wearing a blazer or something that had a shitload of buttons on it; there was a long skirt, a pair of boots with a large heel.

Bog bodies showed up every couple of years around here. We'd seen the pictures in the papers. They were from centuries ago, whores and heathens strung up by the locals because they didn't believe in the right God. Or because they didn't believe in God the right way. They were fully preserved by the salts in the marsh, complete with skin and clothes. Their hair was parted however they parted it during their time on earth.

I saw Kika and Chucho walking down the 12th fairway with a couple of shovels.

"Dutty went into town," Chucho said. "At least that's what I think Kika just told me."

Kika was wearing cutoff shorts and a tank top and her hair was up in a ponytail. She was barefoot and I noticed that she'd painted her toenails black.

"There's a body," I explained, pointing at my feet. "And Chucho and I are going to dig it out."

I was speaking slow and loud, hoping that Kika might gain some meaning from my enunciation and volume.

Kika responded in Russian. I heard her say the word "Dutty" and then she spit on the ground. She said his name again and spit. "Dutty," she said. Then she spit three more times right in a row.

"Lady," I told her. "We understand. Dutty sucks. We get it."

After she was out of spit, Kika flopped down on the edge of the marsh and lit another cigarette. Chucho passed me a shovel and we started digging. After about ten minutes we'd cleared the wet earth around the body. Chucho took the legs and I grabbed onto the shoulders and we lifted it out and set it down on the shore.

It was a woman. Her skin was this strange silvery metallic color. She was wearing a long skirt and a waistcoat that buttoned all the way up to her chin. Her hair was pulled back into a bun.

When Kika realized what we'd pulled out of the marsh, she started screaming and pointing at the body. Then she started screaming and pointing at us. Who knows what she thought? Maybe that we were teenage murderers who liked to dig up our kills and show them to our next victims. Maybe she'd already had enough of this place, enough of Dutty. Her shrieking was tremendous, and it scared the nesting herons and the endangered reticulated wood owls in the marsh up into flight. Chucho moved toward her to calm her down, but when she saw him coming at her, Kika screamed again and then she ran off.

Chucho and I watched her run down the road toward town, wondering if we should stop her, try to explain this. Maybe there was some diagram we could sketch out that would help her understand that this sort of thing was normal around here. But neither of us moved a muscle. We were both tired of Dutty too, sick of having to give him more money than we thought he deserved.

"If he wants her," Chucho said. "Let him go track her ass down."

- - - - - - - -

When Dutty returned a little while later, we showed him the bog body. He got on the phone and called it in. In a few minutes, the town's newspaperman was out at the golf course interviewing us.

He posed us next to the bog body and snapped pictures. We pointed and smiled.

"You seen Kika?" Dutty asked me.

"Haven't," I told him.

He gave me a little nod and then he turned and trudged back up the 12ᵗʰ fairway. That day would be the last time any of us ever saw Kika, and it seemed like Dutty already knew that she had disappeared. He was walking up that hill like he was an old man who did not trust the earth to hold his weight. He was walking like there was something strange buried beneath the soles of his feet and for the life of him he couldn't seem to figure out what it was.

.

FLIGHT PATH

I hear the elevator doors open. The wheels of a hospital bed bump down the linoleum and I run over to the tiny window in my reinforced door. There is a man covered in tubes, lying on a stretcher by the nurses' station.

"Look!" I yell to my roommate, Erica. "Look, look, look!"

Erica gets out of her bed and stands on her tiptoes next to me. We are both patients at The Terrence and Miriam Wexler Wellness Center and Spa, located on the top floor of the County Hospital. The Wellness Center is actually a women's psych ward. They call it a "spa" to make us feel better about ourselves. Other than our psychiatrist, Dr. Molina, we have not seen another man up close in a month.

We are supposed to be focusing our energy on ourselves; we are supposed to be turning inward, owning up to the particular problems that plague us. We are supposed to be making sustainable life changes that can actually be sustained. We are not supposed to be worrying about mysterious, unconscious men who have olive skin and large biceps.

"What's he doing here?" Erica asks.

I look at the man—his head held in a metal halo, his leg cast up to his hip. I watch as they roll him into the room across the hall from us.

"He's here," I tell Erica, "to fall in love."

The man's name is Mike Phipps. He is in a coma. I check this fact about fifty times. I plod over in my pink robe and my paper mules and peruse his chart whenever the nurses aren't looking. Mike Phipps. I keep checking his name each time I go into his room, even though I know it hasn't changed. Mike Phipps. I want to make sure. Mike Phipps. I can't stop.

Mike Phipps's eyes are closed, but he is nowhere near dead. The nurses treat him like he's nearly gone, bandying his limbs with little interest, wetting his dark hair into a mohawk and then bringing the other nurses in to laugh.

"Wake up, sleepyhead," they tell him. "Rise and fucking shine."

I find out from Charlotte, one of the float nurses, that all the beds in the hospital below us are full and this is where Mike will stay until something opens up.

"He's here for now," she tells me. "A little treat for all of us."

Charlotte leaves and I stay with Mike. I comb his hair back down to normal. I wet a washcloth in the sink and I press it down on his forehead.

"Don't worry," I say. "We'll take great care of you."

I slip my hand into his. It's easy. No one notices, no one sees. I slide the chair closer to him and lean in and kiss him lightly on the forehead. I peek out into the hall. No one is coming so I give him a kiss on the lips, lightly at first and then shoving my tongue through. I can feel his teeth. I whisper in his ear.

"There's more where that came from," I say.

- - - - - - - -

Mike Phipps has a girlfriend, Lily. Lily comes in the afternoon, this tiny Filipino thing in swishy pants, her hair shiny like videotape.

"*He* made this," she says to me, pointing to Mike Phipps and then to her belly. "It's a girl. I checked."

I would never have guessed Lily is pregnant. Her body is hidden in bagginess—those running pants, an oversized hoodie underneath a pea coat. She offers me a handshake, her hand darting from her sleeve like a baby bird snatching a grub from a mother's beak. I notice her tattoo then, the name "Mike" running down the side of her neck.

"You are going to regret that," I tell her. "Boy oh boy are you going to regret that."

At first Lily looks at me like I'm crazy, but then her face softens and her lips un-purse. I figure that one of the nurses has prepped her about what she might encounter on our floor. I can tell by the look in her eyes that whatever anger she has for me has now been trumped by pity.

"I won't regret it," she says.

I lift up my shirt to show Lily my regrets, the names of seven men I have loved. I did not think any of these men were going to leave me when I got their names tattooed on my body, but they did leave, one after another. I tried, with limited success, to cover up their names with a new tattoo of a rose or a butterfly. Now my body looks like an English garden, but one grown only to cover a tagged-up wall.

"That's incredible," Lily says.

I pull down my shirt and walk over to Mike's window. I watch a plane descend from the clouds, teeter and list toward the runway lights, bump down and slow to a crawl. The hospital is located by an international airport and planes drop from the sky every fifteen minutes or so. The first couple of weeks here it terrified me, but now that my fear has subsided I've become annoyed with it. It's difficult to change one's habits with the hubbub of an airport in such close proximity. At least that is what I keep telling Dr. Molina.

"He had an accident," Lily says to me. "In case you were wondering."

I turn back to look at Mike Phipps. He is hooked up to tubes and colored wires and everything makes annoying beeping sounds. His head is circled in bandages. Still, I can't stop looking at him. He has a couple days of stubble. And those arms! They look like they could surround a person, trap them inside and never ever let them go.

"He got wasted the night I told him about the baby," Lily says. "Drove his car into a bridge."

Lily's eyes scan from my feet to my face, up and back down. I recently put on some weight and all the clothes I brought with me are being pushed to their limits. I haven't showered in a day or two. I cut my own hair a couple of months ago and it has grown back in a weird bob that sits on my head like a crooked pith helmet.

"Can I ask you why you're here?" she asks. "Is that allowed?"

I turn back to the tarmac. I watch the plane that just landed taxi toward its gate. There is a constant muttering of turbines around us, and people floating above our heads, on vacation or business, visiting loved ones, poised to start a better life in some brand new city. They are taxiing, taking off, circling, about to land. I imagine they look down on us from the sky and marvel at our size, compare us to some type of small, squash-able bug.

"I'm here because I beat somebody's ass," I say.

I'm lying to Lily, trying to scare her. The reason that I'm really here is because I can't stop taking knives and cutting up my skin. It's a young person's thing, something I read about in a glossy magazine and then tried because I wanted to feel younger. I didn't think much about it until I tried it, but then I was shocked at how good it felt. It felt like the old me had melted away and there was a new and better person climbing out from the gunk, a feeling that I loved and wanted to feel nearly once an hour for a period of a couple of weeks, which had subsequently ruined all my sheets and towels and left me dangerously short of blood.

I tell Lily this lie about beating someone up and I decide to make it look convincing. I take my hand and make it into a fist and start pounding it down into my other palm as hard as I can. My fist makes a flat slapping sound that echoes throughout Mike Phipps's room. I probably should have told Lily that I had kidney disease or cervical cancer. I should have told her that I had something that would've made me look more sympathetic, but I just keep on pounding my fist into my hand, harder and harder until it becomes red and starts to sting, another feeling that I can't help loving.

"I beat somebody's ass *bad*," I say.

I find out from Erica that if you bribe Charlotte with a nicotine patch, she will unlock your door for you at night. I find out that for two more, she'll key you into Mike's room.

"Personally I like my men with a bit more spunk," she tells me. "But it's your nicotine."

Tonight, I push aside all the wires and tubing and I climb into Mike's bed. I curl my body up against his. I run my fingers under his hospital gown. I press my ear up to his mouth.

"Liz," I hear him tell me, "I love your hot ass."

Mike's voice is a low and guttural grunt, barely audible. Sometimes the words Mike whispers aren't really words; sometimes they are just phlegm or his teeth grinding together, but I make up words for him.

"Liz," I hear him say tonight, "you are a beautiful woman with personality to spare."

I take Mike's hand and stroke his fingers up and down my thigh.

"Nice," I tell him.

I make him grab a handful of my hair and pull.

"Uh-huh," I say.

I take his index finger and his thumb and I put them on my nipple and squeeze.

"Oh," I moan.

This hospital is not a spa, but the staff still get pissed if you don't use its entire name—"The Terrence and Miriam Wexler Wellness Center and Spa"—whenever you refer to it. When we are alone, Erica and I call it whatever we want.

"Spa?" Erica yells. "Who ever heard of a spa with suicide watch? Who ever heard of a spa being a stone's throw from a fleet of airbuses bound for Baltimore? They have massages at a spa. Where's my fucking massage? Where's my cleansing tea? Spa, my bunghole."

Erica says the word "bunghole" a lot. She's the same age as me, forty-one, and of all the words she uses "bunghole" is probably her favorite. Saying the word "bunghole" a lot is not why she is here, though. Erica is here because she swallows everything she sees. She used to be a corporate accountant and she says this is the reason why she likes swallowing office supplies—pens, binder clips, rubber bands—more than anything else. Still, given the opportunity, Erica will swallow just about anything that fits into her mouth.

"I just ate an entire *Vogue* magazine," she tells me when I walk back into our room.

Erica is my best friend here, but she's a real piece of work. A week ago, one of the day nurses, Sharon, left her wedding ring out at the nurse's station and Erica got her hands on it. For the next two days, Sharon suffered through the indignity of having to poke around in our toilet with a wooden ruler.

"If I don't find it," she told us, "my husband will kill me. Seriously. No joke. He hasn't noticed yet, but for the four months of his salary he put up to buy that rock, he will definitely kill and dismember. I'll be sitting in cold storage right next to his deer meat."

Erica was sorry, but realistic.

"Sharon knows my motto," she told me. "Finders, swallowers— losers, wallowers."

Incredibly, after two days of checking in our toilet, Sharon found her wedding ring glinting up at her in the blue water. She grabbed it and jumped up and down and then gave both Erica and me hugs.

"Good as new," she said after she rinsed it off. She held it up to the light to make sure and then slipped it back on her finger. She had the face of someone who was telling herself something that she didn't truly believe. "Good as ever, right?"

I have seen Erica devour a box of staples like they were a stack of Pringles. I have seen her eat an entire institutional size jar of mayo with her bare hands. I have seen her break apart a digital camera with a teensy hammer and then savor it slowly, piece by tiny electronic piece, then swallow the little hammer for dessert. Every time she comes out of the bathroom, she lies down on the bed and tries to catch her breath. It is so damn hard on her insides, passing all of this stuff, but she can't stop. She's told me that she isn't only addicted to the swallowing now, that she's addicted to the attention. Her habit is her press hook. The thing that is hurting her is the thing that sets her apart from the rest of the world.

Lily is by Mike's bedside when I go into his room after lunch today. All she does is sit, heavy lidded, stumped as to what to do. A lot of the time, she stares out the window and looks down on the parking lot. Sometimes she narrates the comings and goings of different kinds of cars to him.

"Honda Civic," she says. "Some kind of Lexus, I think."

Other than this, she never really talks to Mike. She never tells him about what they are going to do when he wakes up. She never sings songs to him. She sits in the chair by the window, eating M&Ms that she pulls one by one from her coat pocket and stuffs into her tiny mouth.

"He had a car that he loved," she tells me today. "That one he crashed. He was always out on the driveway underneath the hood. I think he loved that damn car way more than he loved me."

I want to tell Lily that I know about men and their cars. I want to tell her how they hide under the hoods, how they always need just five more minutes to ratchet something down. How that five minutes turns into an hour, how one of their buddies stops by and that five minutes turns into the rest of the night and they drink beer under a garage light too dim to even attract bugs.

"I've been down that street," I say.

Lily reaches into her purse now, hands me a picture. It's her and Mike, leaning against a car that has a skull and crossbones painted on the hood. They are both laughing. Mike has his arm around her. He's wearing a backwards baseball hat. Lily's got braces; she's wearing a blue tank top with a picture of a dolphin jumping up out of the waves.

"That's the car," she tells me. "That's us."

I hand the picture back to her even though I have a strong urge to rip it right down the middle, crumple her part up and put the part with Mike safely in my pocket. I know I could find some glue or some Scotch tape around here. I could get someone to take a picture of me. I could slide Mike Phipps and me together into a silver frame and I could tell everyone that this was the man who would finally stand by my side.

"Do you get off on seeing me sad or something?" Lily asks me. "Is that why you keep coming?"

I stare out at the runway. There's a baggage handler in the distance, throwing suitcases into the cargo hold of a plane. He's throwing them as fast as he can, really putting his back into it. It looks like he's done, but then another luggage tram drives up and he starts all over again.

"I'm here to help," I tell Lily.

Most nights, I massage Erica's shoulders and we play a game we call "What We Want Most."

"The thing I want most is a real cigarette," she tells me. "I would trade just.about anything for a real goddamn cigarette."

Here at the Spa, we can't smoke and so everyone uses the patch. We rub our patches like maniacs, hoping that the nicotine will release into our bodies on our schedule. Dr. Molina tells us that it doesn't happen like that, he tells us it is a timed release, that we can't just force the stuff out of the patch whenever we want. We never listen to Dr. Molina. We never listen to him when he tells us to journal about our hopes and fears; we never listen to him when he asks us to tell him what is on our minds. We rub our nicotine patches like we haven't heard a single word he's said.

One night last week, Trudy, one of the girls here, stole a huge stash of patches from the nurses' station and slapped them onto her body into a makeshift bikini.

"Woo-hoo!" she yelled. She was jumping around like it was spring break or something. "All right! Woo!"

We all stood around and admired her as she strutted down the hall at breakneck speed. She was using the hall as a catwalk and she couldn't stop talking—blabbing on about her old boyfriend, about her hometown, about how she used to go to the beach all the time and wore a real bikini, not a fake one made of nicotine patches. After about five minutes of jumping around, she turned green and started puking. The nurses came and carted her downstairs to the emergency room. For a while, there was a rumor that Trudy had died, but then yesterday she came back to group, unrepentant, ready to do it all over again.

"I thought that my heart was going to explode," she told Dr. Molina. "I was so damn excited about being alive. Who feels like that anymore? You tell me who."

I dig my fingers into Erica's shoulders now. She is surprisingly supple for eating so much metal and plastic.

"That bunghole Molina keeps telling me that I want a baby," she tells me. "That I'm trying to fill up a void in my body by swallowing everything I see."

Erica talks a lot about her ticking clock, how every day the clock gets closer to snapping into a million pieces, which in the end she would probably eat.

"Molina keeps telling me the same thing," I tell her. "That I cut myself because I want a baby."

No one has ever told me anything about a baby. They tell me that I need to finally admit that cutting myself is a problem. They tell me that this is a cry for help and whether I know it or not this was just the way I thought people would hear me the best. They tell me I was smart to ask for help, but that I asked for help in the wrong way. Ask for help in a way that you don't hurt yourself, the women in the group tell me. Ask for help with your voice instead of with a paring knife.

"A baby," I say to Erica. I start to laugh. This is very funny to me, a baby. I laugh a little too hard about my lie and accidentally fall out of my chair. Dee-Dee, one of the float nurses, is standing outside the lounge and sticks her head in.

"That looked like it hurt," she says.

Erica and I sometimes watch Dee-Dee with her boyfriend. He is a security guard at the hospital. She waits for him in the parking lot and he drives up in a black security van. He slides open the side door of the van and Dee-Dee gets in. The van rocks a little. Fifteen minutes later they get out and we watch them straighten their clothes and pat down their hair. Then they go back to work. It is like this almost every night, so simple, nothing like a coma or a pregnant girl in the way of their good time.

"Just go," I tell Dee-Dee. "I'm fine."

Dee-Dee doesn't leave though; she comes into the room and sits down next to us. She pulls a nicotine patch from her pocket and slaps it on her forearm and takes a deep breath out.

"I heard you were doing better," she says to Erica. "I heard a rumor that they might send you home."

That makes Erica laugh. After a few seconds of laughing, her laugh morphs into a cough. She's covering her mouth and then all the sudden she spits something out into her hand. She opens her palm and sitting there is a AA battery.

"Really?" she says. "I'm going home?"

In group today, it is my turn to share. I start out sharing about how the summer is the worst time to be a cutter, how you have to wear long sleeves to hide the cuts, how it's always so hot wearing long sleeves. I pull back my sweatshirt and flip over my arms. I hold them out to the group, show them the fat pinkish scabs that look like worms on the sidewalk after a heavy rain.

"That other person," I say, "the cutter? That's not the real me."

Dr. Molina sits across from me, stroking his beard. Dr. Molina is a milder-looking Antonio Banderas, shorter pony tail, wider nose, millimeters from gorgeous. He has great lips, big and supple and what I would call giving. Like he might let you kiss them, instead of bearing down on you and forcing you to kiss like he wanted.

"What are you doing to cope with your triggers?" he asks.

I look around the room. We all sit in a circle in orange fabric chairs that make our asses sweat. Sometimes I wonder who sat here before us, sweated in kind. Where are they now? What are they doing with their lives?

"Lately when I want to cut, I focus on another physical sensation," I say. "Like that lady suggested."

Last week a woman came to our group to demonstrate different coping strategies. She showed us how you could slash at a plastic bottle or an old shirt, how you could rip a phone book in half or stomp around in heavy shoes until the need to hurt yourself disappeared.

"That sounds good," Dr. Molina says. "But can you share the exact things you're doing?"

I glance at Erica. She knows what I've been doing. She's sees me leave each night. She sees me walk down the hall to Mike's room. She knows that I take his hands and press them all over my body until the feeling to cut is gone.

"Yesterday when I wanted to cut, I took an ice cube and I held it in my palm," I say. "And by the time the ice had melted the feeling had disappeared."

When group is over, Dr. Molina stands next to the door and hands out pieces of butterscotch hard candy.

"Liz, can you come to my office for a second?" he asks me.

Everyone here is curious what Dr. Molina's life is like when he leaves the hospital. Behind his desk, mounted on the wall above his head, are framed pictures of him in action—running a marathon in Hawaii, milking a cow in India. The one I like best is him climbing to the summit of KB2. He's gripping a flag that he's just shoved into the mountain. He's wearing thick black gloves and his beard is covered in frost. It all looks satisfying and violent, his arms pushing that flagpole deep into the crusty snow.

"I could never do that," I tell him, pointing at the picture. "I've got a pair of weak lungs."

"You could," he says. "You just need to prepare properly."

I want to believe him, but I know not to. I take my piece of hard candy and spin it open. I put it into my mouth, feel the sugar leak down the back of my throat.

"Mike Phipps's girlfriend tells me you've been a real help," he says.

I bite down on the hard candy and it shatters inside my mouth. I stick out my tongue to look at the tiny shards.

"I am trying to save her some heartache," I say.

Dr. Molina goes into his desk drawer. He pulls out four nicotine patches and slides them across his desk.

"Whatever you are doing," he says "keep it up."

The next afternoon, I find Lily curled up in a chair by Mike's bed. The nurses have just given him a sponge bath and the room smells like apple.

"I take the bus here," Lily says. "And I am so sick of it. Everyone on the bus keeps touching my stomach. Old ladies, kids, whoever. I try to hide from them but somehow they know I'm pregnant. They just walk up and start pawing."

She leaves Mike and moves over to me, grabs my hand. It's moist. It feels strange, like there aren't any bones inside. I can't stop thinking about the way I rake her boyfriend's fingers over my body, forcing him to scratch me until I feel right again.

"I'm losing him," she says. "He's dead, but then he won't really die."

I stare at Mike, wanting to pull the sheets aside, take in his entire body.

"He's going to wake up," I tell her. "You just need a little faith."

Sometimes it looks like Mike is smiling, a sliver of a tooth showing through his lips. I want to tell him to quit. I want to say to him: *not now.*

"I brought you something," Lily says. She moves over to the side of the bed and hands me a silver box with a bow on it.

"What is this for?" I ask.

"It's just because," she says.

I don't get presents "just because." The boyfriends whose names I tattooed into my skin rarely gave me anything. If they did, they gave me things that were clearly presents for them. A box of steaks, lingerie, a set of men's golf clubs.

"Just open it," she says.

I slide off the ribbon and pull back the tissue paper. It's a new robe—light blue, terrycloth, beautiful and soft, and I lift it up and it unfurls.

A feeling comes over me then, a churning emptiness in my stomach. I put the robe back into its box and I set it down on the floor. I take my arms and I wrap them around my belly. I burp and the burp tastes like puke.

"Try it on," she says.

"Later," I say.

"No way," she says. "Try it on now."

I shake my head no, but Lily lifts the robe and gets me to stand up. She slides the terrycloth over the clothes I am wearing and she ties the sash around my waist.

"There we go," she says. "That looks great."

And even though there are no mirrors here, even though I can't really see what it looks like, I can tell that she's done a great job. I can tell that it fits.

That night, after visitor's hours are over, I bribe Charlotte and I sneak back into Mike's room again.

"You're wicked," Charlotte tells me before I enter. "But I still like you."

"This is my substitute," I say. "Some people use cigarettes. Or drink coffee."

"I don't judge," she says. "Knowing what I know, I never judge."

Charlotte has a bad limp. From what Erica and I have heard it's from her former husband, who pushed her off a third floor balcony and then left her for dead. Who knows if that's true, I think. Maybe she just has a bad hip. Maybe that's the extent of it. Maybe it's just genetics. Maybe it was passed down from the combination of her mother and father getting together and there was nothing anyone could have done.

I stand by the side of Mike's bed. There's a thin stream of drool running out the side of his mouth. I smell urine under everything that is trying to cover up the smell of urine.

"What are you waiting for?" I hear him ask me.

I pull the sheets back, but instead of getting in bed, I stop and stare at his body. How long will it take before it wastes away? A week, a month? How long before all the muscle disappears and his skin pulls tight against his bones?

"C'mon," he whispers. "Let's do this."

His calves have shed their hair and they look thin and grey. His face is blotchy. I take my fingers and I gently pull open both of his eyelids. I shake my head back and forth in front of his rolling eyes.

"This has to stop," I say.

On the way back from breakfast the next morning, Lily sees me outside her room and grabs my hand and pulls me in. Mike is propped up in his bed wearing a paper crown that says "Congratulations." There is a big cookie in the shape of a heart on the bedside table. The cookie is no longer intact. Lily has started in on it, her little hand cleaving a piece from the butt end of the heart.

"The baby is really craving chocolate today," she says.

She takes another piece of cookie and shoves it into her mouth.

"I figured we could celebrate," she says. "I needed something—you know? Even if he doesn't care."

She breaks off a piece of the cookie and hands it to me. "They're moving him today," she says.

"Moving him?" I ask.

"There's a bed open," she says, "downstairs."

I get up and move over to the window. Instead of looking out, I watch Lily's reflection in the glass. I see the tears welling up in her eyes, getting ready to fall. I watch her wrap her arms around her stomach. We are quiet for a minute, chewing. I start rubbing the nicotine patch on my shoulder. I want to tell her that we are in love with the same man, that we are doing the same thing, just trying to use that feeling to get through the day.

"Sometimes he whispers," I say.

She nods. She tells me she knows. "I can never understand what he's saying."

"I can." I turn to look at her. "I know what he's saying."

I tell her that I heard Mike say he is happy to be starting a family. That I heard him say Lily is going to be a great mom. How they are going to buy a house and get a dog—a big lazy dog.

I say all these things to her and she starts to cry. Then she points to her stomach.

"Tell her," she says.

I am reluctant, but I sit down next to Lily and I lean over and she pulls up her shirt and I put my lips there. And I start talking. Her skin is slippery with cocoa butter, but there's a bit of salt, a bit of sweat underneath. I tell the baby what I've just told Lily. And then I keep going. I tell the baby other things. I feel a stirring under my lips, a shifting wave moving across the tautness of her belly. I do not stop. I keep talking even when a plane passes overhead and everything that I am saying is turned into something fierce and hissing. I say everything I know into her belly and when I run out of words I just start to hum.

I hear babies like that.

MAIL GAME

I was playing this mail game with a girl at work.

Hot potato, basically.

Except it was with this two-dollar bill.

Back and forth. Back and forth. Ha ha.

Neither of us wanted the damn thing. We hid it everywhere. Once, she found it in her underwear drawer at her house. That excited and bothered her.

Jimmy, she said, you are pretty damn sneaky.

At the same time all that was happening, I finished learning Spanish.

I had wanted to become a flight attendant—bouncing over the ocean, digging my toes back into solid land. The airline said Spanish would help.

Nope.

Look at you—they said to me during an interview—you are one huge mofo. You are way too big to go up, they said.

I still had all these post-it notes with vocab words stuck all over my place. The Spanish word for trash can—*cubo de basura*. The word for knife, *cuchillo*.

Those are the ones I could not forget.

During that summer, people came over and ate my food and drank my wine and tried to pronounce things off the post-it notes and even though I hated Spanish now, I corrected them.

Cuchillo, I would say.

Then slower. Cu-CHEE-yo, not cuch-ILLO.

See the difference? I would say.

Escucha y repita, I told them.

They left angry, my guests. They called me a pompous ass and kicked the sand candles that lighted my sidewalk.

The girl at work and I finally married.

I told her I might crush her one day.

Really? she said.

Really, I said.

I am so large and you are so tiny, so probably it will happen, I told her.

Really? she said.

One night, rolling around naked, we found some coins in our bed.

Who knows about these things?

They could have come from anywhere, far away, so close, pockets. They weren't like a dollar bill. You write your name on a dollar bill and pay for something and someday when it returns to your wallet you can say—see, see, I told you so.

These were coins, though, coins, maybe ours to begin with and maybe not.

GRAVITY

Call it a hobby.

Call it a hobby because a hobby is for utter enjoyment, right? And since there is nothing more enjoyable for you than to see someone brained with a small metal object, this is your hobby. You do not collect Hummels, you are not one of those scary autograph hounds shoving kids out of your way for a second of communion with celebrity, you don't buy expensive retrospective toys trying feebly to rediscover your fleeting youth.

You drop small denomination coins on people standing on the street below.

Bonk.

You drop these coins from the eighteenth floor where your office is, from the law firm where you are a newly minted partner. The windows up here shouldn't ever open, but they do if you know the trick.

There is always a trick. Sometimes you need to ask around to find out what that trick is, but there always is one. It turns out that in this case the trick is a tool. Pavel from Maintenance gave one to you. The tool looks like a crowbar, but skinnier and without the teeth. Pavel shoved it into this hole at the base of the window and twisted it like a screwdriver and the window spun magically open.

"This for instance, Mr. Stone?" Pavel asked you in his halting English. "For instance, fire? For instance, you need to jump safe?"

You and Pavel have talked about "for instances" before. You've been a "for instance" kind of guy from way back, you prefer when people have questions about what *could* happen, how things *could* go horribly wrong.

"Yes," you tell Pavel. "Of course. Another for instance."

Pavel is here all the time, not lurking or anything, but inconvenient just the same. You think everyone has left for the night and you are just about to drop a coin onto someone below when you hear his mop bump into the snack machine in the break room.

"In case of the fires, right?" Pavel asks you.

"Exactly," you tell him. "Jump. Jump instead of burn."

You've had things hit you on the head too. Once you had a bagel hit you on the top of the head in the middle of the street. It was late and you were drunk and tired and on your way to the train station. There was no one on the street, no cars, a nasty steam billowing up from the sewer. Then, out of nowhere, this bagel. After it nailed you, you looked up and pondered the skies. You yelled, "Hello?" When you slowly realized no one was going to cop to throwing this hard-ass bagel, you yelled, "Fuck!"

Who wouldn't? You are no different than anyone else. A bagel hits you on the head—that is what you do. You look toward the heavens and see how this happened, see if someone will accept the blame. You quiet yourself, still the raucous pounding of your heart in your ears, hope that at the very least you hear someone giggle.

You got the idea for the pennies after the bagel. You call

the bagel "inspiration" because you actually went home and brainstormed some ideas about what to throw. You wrote your ideas down on a yellow legal pad at your desk in the basement, crossed some of them out, circled a couple.

"Yes!" you yelled when you came to the word "Coins." "Hell yes!" It was a boisterous yell, something that could have easily accompanied a karate kick. It was exciting and you actually got out of your chair, did this little jig, spiked your pencil onto the floor in a celebration of your brilliance.

"What are you doing down there?" your wife asked you over the intercom.

"Behind at the office," you lied.

"Bullshit," she said. "I heard cackling."

"Just need to finish one last report," you told her.

Ah, your wife Jeannie. You still love her. You still love her like you loved her before. That is what you tell her. And of course, you try so damn hard to love her the same. You know that is the way it should be. Love doesn't disappear when someone is bedridden. That is what you tell yourself. You tell yourself that sometimes love just hides away from the light for a while. And right now in your life, you think, this is a point where love is hiding. That is what you tell yourself even though you don't really know if that is the truth or if love will ever (peek-a-boo!) show itself again.

Before her accident, Jeannie was a teacher in this public school in the city. You remember how she brought home these stories. Stories about a kid shoving a pocketknife in another kid's ear. Stories about kids opening their lockers and guns clattering out onto the floor. There was always gossip in the teacher's lounge about what strange thing set off the metal detector today (His braces? Really?), about who was sleeping with who (The math teacher? With that slutty speech clinician?).

Jeannie loved her job, let it burrow inside her. All the pain she dealt with should have blackened her mood, but all she wanted to do when she got home was fuck, a byproduct of being around all of those kids' boundless energy.

"I am burning up, my skin is on fire, I am dripping wet, please please do me," she used to moan right after she walked in the door.

She stripped down to nothing, crawled over to you in the recliner, this trail of teacher clothes—blouses and long skirts—laid in her wake.

She especially liked sex from high places. On top of tables, suspended over staircases. One time on vacation in rural Connecticut you did it on a trestle bridge looking over a stony brook, and another time when you were house sitting you snuck up to the roof of your friend's brownstone and held her body over the building's edge. You made her feel like she was falling and then you reached out and caught her right before she actually fell.

"Again," she always said and you always obliged.

Then came the first time you dropped her. She didn't specifically ask you to do it, but you knew that she wanted you to let it happen at least once, right? You'd been feeling the excitement in your marriage slide away little by little and by now you felt that it had gotten all too familiar, a ride that she knew would never go off the rails. One night, you let her fall about ten feet from the staircase down into the front entry and she hit the floor. Hard.

There was that second when you stared down at her from the stairs, legs akimbo, arms askance, shocked at what you'd done. Jesus. Was your life going to be different from this point forward? Were you going to spend some time in jail? You were amazed when she stood up and brushed herself off.

"That was really hot," she said. "Wow."

After that, she *demanded* to be dropped. You didn't want to do it after that first time, but she kept begging and pleading and sometimes you complied. Obviously you were always nervous about it, but months passed and all that ever happened when you dropped her were these bruises—black and blue knots that after a while turned dark brown and then yellowed and finally disappeared.

"People are going to think I beat you," you told her.

"People are going to think whatever it is they always think," she told you. "No matter what you and I do."

Of course one day it went badly. You dropped her from the deck and she landed awkwardly on her arm. She got up and it was just dangling there, her forearm flopping around like a boiled noodle.

"I can't do this anymore," you told her after you'd driven her to the hospital and she had lied to the doctor in the emergency room—said she'd fallen rollerblading. "We need to find something else that's exciting to you. We've got to be done with this."

"There isn't anything else," she said. "This is what I like. This is how I like it."

"You'll get hurt way worse than this," you told her.

"I don't care," she said.

It is Thursday night and Thursday is one of the nights that you put all the expensive oils and bubble beads into Jeannie's bath. Your back is killing you and you have to wear a weight belt to lift her. You've gotten used to the piece of leather around your waist and sometimes you wear it even at work now, just for the little extra support it gives. You can't really see it under your shirts and sweaters, but some of your office mates found out about it and they've started to give you the business.

"Just back from the gym, Sporto?" they ask.

You do not tell your wife about your co-workers. You used to, but now you save her your problems. She has enough of her own. She can still wash herself, but you sit on the edge of the tub and talk to her. You are happy she is still washing herself. There might come a day when washing is another one of your jobs, but you are glad that it is not now.

"I'm sorry," she tells you again tonight. "I don't know how you can ever forgive me."

"It's my fault, too," you say. You don't really want to believe that fact, but there is a reason that actuary tables exist, a reason that insurance company's formulas can assign fault to simply being present at a certain map point at a certain time.

"We're fine," you tell her.

Sometimes at night though, lying in bed, you can't get the thoughts of her with that other man out of your head, the science teacher from her school, the one who you met at the hospital, the blond-haired one with the cleft chin who was with her when she fell that last time and then didn't get up.

"You know I still loved you when that happened," Jeannie tells you as you lift her out of the tub. "You know that wasn't what it was about, right?"

Most people are perplexed when it happens. Things falling from above have always perplexed people. Some forget that the sky is an easy option for violence, that the heavens can open up on you at a moment's notice. When it happens, you'd like to think that God had something to do with it, that there is a plausible explanation, that if you looked up there would be someone there waving and yelling, "My fault!"

You throw one coin. Never more. More would be a pattern. Something to figure out. Something to track back to its source.

You stay late at the office on Friday, waiting for your chance. It is like masturbating when you were younger; you knew that if you didn't do it you wouldn't feel right for the rest of the day. So you wait as the office staff files out, as the partners leave for the night.

"Your billable hours are putting us to shame, Sporto," they say.

You hear Pavel whistling down the corridor, some happy working song, he's not finished yet either. He stops by your office to chat and then he won't leave. He tells you about his weekend plans—he's helping move his cousin into a new apartment and he's going to church. You listen, even ask the few questions. You are distracted, though. You keep glancing over at the window. Yes, yes, you nod, what a life.

"Can I ask question?" Pavel says.

"Go ahead," you say.

"I ask this because I need to know," he says.

"Ask away," you tell him.

You are still staring out the window. You are sitting up high enough here that sometimes you are actually *part* of the weather, low flying clouds sometimes engulf the building, occasionally you see lightning snaking from cloud to cloud.

"Your wife," Pavel asks you, "how hard is?"

When you get home that night, Jeannie is there waiting for you. She's lying in bed; the nurse you have hired for the daytime hours has just left. You sit down next to her, notice that she's all dolled up, wearing makeup. Her hair is pulled back into a ponytail; she's wearing a low-cut shirt.

"What's the occasion?" you ask.

"No occasion," she tells you.

"There must be something," you say.

"Nope," she says.

She pats the bed twice and you move over and sit next to her. She takes her hand and snakes it in under your shirt. She untucks you, unbuckles your belt.

"I'm fine," you say.

She slides her hand into your boxers.

"You don't have to do this," you tell her.

You were only being polite, you need this, you need this badly, you are rock hard, shifting your hips into her hand.

"That's what I'm talking about," she says. "Uh-huh."

You'd forgotten that this was a possibility. You've forgotten that this was how it was before. You slide up closer to her and she kisses you and unbuttons your shirt. You slide off your pants and you close your eyes and you feel her drop down and take you in her mouth.

Afterward, you help Jeannie back down to her pillow and you lay down next her on the bed. You take her hand in your hand and you turn your head to look at her.

"Thank you," you say.

You both lie like that for a little while, nearly weightless, letting the bed, the floorboards, the house, do their work. You'd forgotten this feeling; you'd forgotten how all of these things cradle your body, how they surround you, how they stop you from being pulled into the center of the goddamn earth.

MAKE-A-WISH

He's a professional baseball player, just not the one I want. The one I wanted to go deep sea fishing with was the shortstop, the one who does the back flip before every game, the master of infield chatter, the guy with the infectious smile and the chain of urban sports bars.

What I get is a designated hitter who once kicked a seagull for fun. His name is Eusebio Urbina and there are rumors.

Isn't it obvious? all the pundits on TV scream, his skull is ginormous, he keeps pulling his hamstrings, his eyes are as yellow as post-it notes.

"Pleased to meet you, Danny," Eusebio says. He holds out his massive hand out for me to shake, but I leave it suspended in mid-air. I spin on my heel, shove a photographer out of my way, and walk up the gangplank to the fishing boat.

"Let's just get this over with," I yell back down.

- - - - - - - -

We troll through the harbor, past all the cruise ships and docked sailboats. It's just the two of us, Eusebio and me, in a huge orange boat that has "Doritos" written all over it. On the hull, on the galley tables, on the steering wheel cover. Doritos. There are bags of Doritos strategically placed on the benches to look like throw pillows. There is a mini-fridge stocked to the gills with sandwiches and pop. There is a fruit and cheese plate the size and shape of a small butte.

"You weren't my wish," I tell Eusebio.

Eusebio sighs. He digs into his duffel bag and yanks out a bottle of dark liquor. He spins the top off, takes a long swallow. He holds the bottle out to me, shakes it back and forth.

"And you weren't mine," he says.

I'm fifteen. According to every oncologist, shaman, and tea leaf reader in the tri-state area that my mother keeps dragging me to, I've got between three and six months to live. Right now, I am wearing a blue shirt that says "Carpe Diem" but I've scratched off the *e* and the *m* so the shirt reads "Carp Die."

I grab the bottle from Eusebio and put it to my lips and take a pull.

We clear the harbor and Eusebio cuts the engine. He's already finished off one bottle of rum and he takes off his shirt and ties it around his head. He scratches his goatee, takes another pull on the new bottle he's just opened.

"You drive," he says. "I'll sleep."

He flops down on one of the benches in the back of the boat, lights up a cigarette. It is hard not to remember back to when Eusebio was hitting everything out of the ballpark. Every time he came up to bat, the place went apeshit. Whenever he hit a home run, he did this complicated dance full of elbow and chest bumps and high fives with the shortstop. I was fine then, not sick at all. Or maybe whatever was inside me had not decided to cause any trouble.

Now, Eusebio hardly ever gets off the bench. Whenever he does there are only heckling and slurs, the occasional syringe chucked at him. The shortstop won't mention him by name in post-game interviews. The shortstop calls him "The Designated Hitter" or "Number 8" like he's forgotten Eusebio's name.

I slide into the captain's chair and start the engine. I yank the throttle down and feel the boat lurch forward. I am drunk and sweaty and I can feel the liquor sloshing around in my gut. Eusebio points to some seagulls.

"A little tip," he tells me as he closes his eyes. "Birds follow fish."

I follow the swooping birds, cut the engine near where they dive down from the clouds. I drop anchor and grab a rod and reel from the compartment under the deck. Even though I'm pretty wasted, I slosh a handful of frozen jumbo shrimp out of the bait box, hook one of them through its gut. I take my rod and rear back, use my entire upper body to cast out. I set the rod into the holder and wait.

Eusebio's snoring. If I had a Sharpie, I'd write something on his forehead. Something like "Cheater" or "I ♥ 'Roid Rage." That's the kind of thing we do all the time at Children's Hospital. Kids wake up with the words "Pillhead" or "Sicko" written on their forehead in permanent marker. The parents never think it is funny, but the kids always find it hilarious, make the nursing staff bring a mirror to their bedside so they can look at it over and over.

I reel in, cast out again.

Eusebio arches his back, rubs his palms over his eyes. He stands up and stumbles over to the edge of the boat. He unzips his pants and cuts a whiz into the ocean.

"Catch anything?" he asks.

I shake my head and Eusebio digs in his bag. The skin on his chest has turned beet red. I assume he's reaching in his bag for another bottle, but instead he holds up a greenish metal orb.

I know right away it is a grenade, but Eusebio is rolling it around in his hand like it's a piece of fruit. He pulls the pin on it with his teeth and then he starts to cackle. I let my rod go, turn and face him.

"Time to stop dicking around," he tells me as he chucks the grenade.

A few seconds later the ocean explodes. This is not my wish either, but it is a brilliant thing to see, a deafening explosion and a shower of sea water misting against our faces. There is a pop, pop, popping sound and I watch as the ocean starts to spit up fish. The surface of the water turns black with them—mackerel and sea bass and bluegill and fish that look like they are from the beginning of time. They have long skinny jaws and big jagged teeth. I take the fishing net and start to scoop them into the boat.

Eusebio jumps into the water and hands fish after dead fish to me. I pile them one on top of the other. First I fill the galley and when I run out of room I pile them on the deck. When that's full, I shove them into the storage areas under the benches, then into the cooler with the soda.

Eusebio gets back into the boat. He opens another bottle of rum, lights up another cigarette. We've been on the high seas for half a day, but I feel like I've been out here for months. I am shirtless and grey with dirt. I am rank with fish. I am drunk on rum and my legs feel like sea legs—rickety and bowed.

I pick at my teeth with a pocket knife and stare toward the horizon. I take a piece of rope and practice knots.

"Are you ready?" Eusebio asks me. His five o'clock shadow has turned into a rough beard; in the moonlight his teeth have a blue tint.

I sit on a bench and I tilt my head back to look up at the sky. The boat is running low on fuel, laboring under our catch. The stars above us are tiny, useless.

MONARCHS

I told Carmen I had a surprise for her. We were at Manny's Good Time and she was lit on gin and juice. She was acting like a little kid, calling me Ricky in this high, squeaky voice. She was sitting on my lap and she had her skinny arms draped around my neck.

"Tell me what it is, Ricky," she said. "Tell me, tell me, tell me."

It was a happy hour and I breathed it all in. There were two-for-ones and free hot wings and Darlene, Manny's wife, was calling out numbers for the meat raffle.

"I can't tell you," I told Carmen. "It's a surprise."

While we sat there, Carmen's hair slid in front of my face. It smelled like apricots. I'd asked her about it once, hoping it was genetic, hoping that it could survive all the bar smoke and beer swill, but she told me that it was just her half-sister's shampoo.

"C'mon," she begged. "Just give me a hint."

I looked Carmen up and down. She was totally my type—too scrawny to have hips, long dark hair, a mouth that was held in a constant sneer.

"You need to learn some patience," I teased. "That's what you need to learn."

Carmen was wearing this low cut black dress and her hair was pulled back into a ponytail. Her skin was nut brown from sitting by the pool at her half-sister Jennie's apartment complex.

I jammed a couple bucks into the jukebox and I led Carmen over near the pool tables. It wasn't really a dance floor, just a spot where the carpet ended, but I pulled her close and twirled her around and around.

"Please," she whispered into my ear.

"Nope," I said.

The next morning I opened the door of my apartment and Carmen rushed past me and ran into my bathroom. She slammed the door closed. I heard her start gagging.

"Hey," I said through the door. "You sick?"

I heard Carmen dry heaving, but then she stopped. The door creaked open. I looked through the crack and saw Carmen slumped over the toilet. Her left hand had gathered up most of her excellent smelling hair, but there were a couple of loose strands hovering dangerously close to the toilet.

"There's something stuck," she said. "There's something stuck in my throat and I can't get it out."

Carmen was younger than me, mid-twenties, but she was fragile. I'd met her two months ago and that first night—when she barely knew me—she told me to take my finger and press down on her arm.

"Why?" I asked.

"Just do it and see what happens," she said.

I pressed my finger down on her arm and the next time I saw her at Manny's, a couple nights later, she showed me the bruise. I had hardly even touched her, but there on her forearm was my fingerprint.

"If you wanted," she told me, "you could do your initials. Or spell out your entire name. You could write whatever you want."

Now Carmen stood in front of my bathroom mirror staring down her throat. She was staying over at my place a couple nights a week now. I'd cleared out a drawer in my dresser and she'd brought over a duffel bag with some clothes. This was as far as I'd gotten with a woman in a long time. I knew that I should savor it, that it was only a matter of time before I did something to drive her away.

"After you dropped me off last night, I fell asleep on Jennie's couch," she said. "This morning I woke up to my little nephew shoving an army man into my mouth."

I went into the kitchen and found a flashlight and pointed it down Carmen's throat. My face was right near her mouth. Whenever she exhaled, there was this annoying sound—like a radiator that needed to be bled.

"Feel right here," she told me.

I put my hand on her throat, felt her swallow. There was something big rattling around in her neck. It could have been just about anything. A wristwatch? Legos? An entire battalion of army men? Who knew what her nephew had found on the floor of that ratty apartment and shoved into her mouth?

"I can't see anything," I told her. "But there's definitely something there."

She turned on the faucet, made a cup with her hands, took a drink.

"Do you want me to take you to the hospital?" I asked.

"No way," she said. She leaned against the sink, ran her hand over her throat, swallowed, then winced. "You said I get a surprise. And I want my goddamn surprise."

The surprise I had for Carmen was that we were driving up north to my father's monarch farm. People needed butterflies for weddings, to christen their babies, for graduation parties. My father was happy to provide this service. He charged five hundred bucks a pop for those ten seconds after he let the butterflies go and the sky turned orange in their honor.

Every year during the first weekend in September, my father went on this trip to visit our relatives in Atlanta. Even though he didn't really trust me, he was too cheap to pay for real help. He gave me a hundred bucks plus gas to look after his place for the weekend.

"Same deal as last time," he told me when he called. "You drive up on Saturday morning, ride back on Sunday morning. That's it. No funny business."

Taking care of the butterflies wasn't hard. Mostly you drank and watched TV. The only thing you ever had to do was turn on the heating lamps if it got too cold.

"Don't be afraid to use those heaters," my father reminded me for the millionth time when he'd called. "There's no shame in using the heaters. No shame at all."

All of the butterflies were housed in this concrete building behind his house. There were tens of thousands of them in there, making their way through their life cycle, from birth to death, but my dad would bitch about even one of them dying. He was a petty man. Once he lectured me for about an hour when he saw that I had accidentally crushed one in the doorframe.

"They're frail," he said. "The slightest touch on their wings and they start flying around in a circle and can't stop. It's horrible to watch."

My father and I went for months at a time without speaking, but whenever he called me in the last few years, the only thing he talked about was monarchs. He told me stats about their migration, tidbits about their place in history, about the things he did to help their pupa production. I suppose this was his attempt to get me more invested, to make me into a better caretaker, but I hardly listened.

"They're an aphrodisiac," he told me. "Henry VIII used to put a butterfly right on the top of his steak."

My father was totally obsessed. It was unhealthy. My mother had left him a long time ago and I was a large disappointment. This was the only thing he had now. These butterflies.

I looked at Carmen as I drove. Her face looked ashen. She kept taking her hands and moving them up and down her throat, trying to figure out what was in there. She pulled a crusty blanket out of the backseat and wrapped it around her shoulders. It was pretty hot out, but she was shivering.

I put my hand on Carmen's knee and squeezed. She was not the first woman I had brought up to my father's place. There were a couple others too. There was this waitress who worked at the Steak 'n' Ale. This girl named Rain who I'd met at the downtown library.

Considering what had happened last time I'd come up here, I was actually surprised that my father had asked me to housesit again. Last time, he'd found a couple of candles inside the shed. Nothing caught on fire, none of his precious butterflies got hurt, but he wouldn't let it rest.

"This isn't a place for you to fuck," he told me.

But it so was. My dad never used it for that, but he should have, because when you stripped naked and laid on the floor in the shed, butterflies floated down and landed all over your naked body. It was an incredible thing. It was like a million tiny lips kissing you all at once. It was insane being in there alone, but with another person to share it with, it was absolutely mind-blowing.

"I need to be able to trust my son," my father told me on the phone. "I need him to understand that my butterflies are not his sex slaves. I need him to understand that they have the same delicate psyches as human beings and they do not like to be involved in your deviant behavior."

"Absolutely," I told him.

I heard him take a deep breath and then blow it out. I'd recently lost a job he'd lined up for me managing a copy shop, and before that I'd gotten fired from his fishing buddy's car dealership. I doubted that he'd stick his neck out for me much longer. I'd just about ruined whatever goodwill that been passed on to me from simply being his son.

"I need you to be responsible," he said.

I knew it was wrong, but as I talked with my father I was already thinking about asking Carmen to come with me. I couldn't help myself. Those butterflies landing on you felt good enough to be disowned.

"I'm your guy," I said.

When I put on the blinker to my dad's house, Carmen's face dropped. There wasn't a lake, there was no carnival, there was no string quartet standing in the driveway. My father lived in a brown rambler and other than the butterfly shed the property had pretty much gone to hell. Next to the house sat a rusted-out school bus that was listing off to one side.

"This is a place you bring someone to kill them," she said. "Is that the surprise? That you've brought me here to die?"

We got out of the car and walked back to the shed. The whistling in Carmen's throat had moved up an octave. I started talking like a carnival barker now, trying to create excitement where there was none.

"There are a million butterflies in there," I explained.

"So what?" Carmen said.

"Have you ever gotten naked and had a million butterflies land on you at once?" I asked her. "It is like being kissed by God. You can't even imagine."

I grabbed onto Carmen's hand, but she pulled it away from me, curled it up into a fist.

"This isn't a surprise," she said. "This is fucked."

- - - - - - - -

When we got inside the house, Carmen locked herself in the bathroom. She sat inside there for two hours. I sat in the basement and watched television until I heard her footsteps upstairs. I found her standing in front of the fridge, holding a picture of my father in her hand. The picture was from a fishing trip a couple of years ago. He was passed out in a hotel bed. Someone had stuck one of those Burger King crowns on his head and drawn a curly mustache on his face in black marker. I wondered if Carmen was going to say that he looked like me. The fact was we did look a lot alike; even with the mustache and the crown it was hard not to notice the resemblance.

"Whose place is this?" she asked.

"It's a friend of mine," I told her. "I help him out sometimes."

I opened up the fridge. I took out a beer and popped it open. I took a pull and passed it to Carmen. She took a drink, grimaced as she swallowed. I opened another one and downed it and then popped open another one and then downed that one too. Then I went into the cabinet and found a candle and a pack of matches.

"Just c'mon," I said. "I promise you'll like it."

I walked outside. Carmen followed a few steps behind. I grabbed the pad off a chaise lounge and dragged it behind me into the shed. For a while, coming in from the outside light, I couldn't see anything. I felt the humid air on my face, heard the massive fluttering of wings above my head. I threw down the pad from the chaise lounge on the floor, lit the candle. In a minute or two, Carmen walked inside, looking sheepish.

"They fly to the ceiling when someone comes in," I explained. "They come down once they get used to us."

I held the candle up near Carmen's face, to try to get an idea of her mood. She was staring up at the ceiling. She didn't look angry any longer and so I moved behind her and started rubbing her shoulders. She spun toward me.

"Fine," she said. "I'm game."

She pulled my shirt over my head. She kicked off her shoes, then stepped out of her shorts. I unbuttoned her shirt.

We started to kiss, but I felt Carmen's body tense up. She pulled away, began to cough.

"Hold on a second," she said.

She put her hand to her throat and she coughed again. Then she gasped and I watched her eyes roll back in her head. She crumpled to the floor.

For a second, I thought Carmen was messing with me. I thought that she was pissed at me for bringing her here. I thought that this was her revenge, getting me excited and then pretending to pass out. When I got down on my knees and put my ears to her mouth, I realized she wasn't joking. She wasn't breathing.

I lifted her up and carried her outside. I took my hands and put them under her ribcage and pulled up. Nothing. She felt cold. Her skin looked grey. I did it again. Her apricot smelling hair was in my eyes and I brushed it away and then I pressed into her ribs again. The third time I did it something flew out of her throat and she began to cough.

I carried her over to the picnic table, set her down. She was shaking. I got a glass of water and a blanket from the house, pressed it around her. She was pointing to the grass. There was a plastic ring with a big red fake jewel there.

"That's what it was," she said.

We sat there, holding each other. I kept asking her if she was alright and she kept telling me that she was fine. She was rubbing her throat and I was trying to come down from the adrenaline rush that someone nearly dying always gives you.

"Look," she said to me then, pointing at the sky. "Look at that."

I looked up and saw that the sky was orange, the monarchs were spilling out of the shed.

"Whoa," Carmen said. "Damn."

I ran over to close the door, but by the time I got there I realized that there was no point in trying to stop what had already started in motion. I sat down in the grass. I watched the butterflies make their way south. I knew my father was done speaking to me regardless of what happened now. All I had left was Carmen.

I went and found the toy ring in the grass and I walked over to her. I knelt down in front of her. Before I could even get the words out of my mouth, before I could tell her how I felt, before I could explain that what had just happened was a sign that we should spend the rest of our lives together, Carmen took off running. This was not what I expected, but it was also exactly what I expected, exactly what she should have done.

"Wait!" I yelled. "Hold on!"

I watched her as she ran across the lawn. She was beautiful. The blanket that she held around her shoulders billowed out around her and made her look like she might float away.

EVERYONE PRANK CALLS THE CLOWN

Everyone prank calls the clown. He's used to it. He's driving home now, having just finished a birthday party for some rich kid with big teeth. The phone number that comes up on his cell says "Unknown." For the most part, the calls the clown gets are from people he does not know. He never lets them roll to voicemail; he answers each and every one. You never know when it might be someone wanting to book him for a birthday party or a mitzvah. You never know when it will be the dognappers contacting him about Choco's ransom.

This time it's teenagers. Teenagers who've seen him driving around wearing his rainbow wig and written down the phone number that's on the door of his clown car. This happens fairly often. Today when the clown answers his phone, there is giggling. The clown pictures a group of girls crowded around a single phone, their ears straining to hear a sliver of his voice.

"Hello?" he says.

"Hahahahahaha," the girls giggle.

These calls do not bother the clown. He is still glad to bring moments of glee and excitement into people's lives. He is still a clown for fucksake.

- - - - - - -

There are other prank calls. Not kids. Late night calls that come while the clown sits on his lime green couch and drinks brandy from a cup that looks like a hollowed-out skull. The clown's wrists, after twenty years of squeaking together balloon animals, feel like they are on fire. His jaw throbs from the millions of smiles he's forced. There is no giggling in these prank calls that the clown gets, there is only an unnerving mechanical groan on the other end of the line. There is only the ripple of static and the occasional deep and fatigued sigh.

"Choco?" the clown yells into the phone whenever he gets one of these calls. "What have you done with Choco?"

The clown never fails to check the animal shelter. Every day for the last six months he has searched the stacked cages for his lost dog. Sometimes he stops by on his way to a birthday party. He's in full makeup and when he crouches down for a closer look at the dogs they lurch out and bare their teeth at him.

"Anyone new?" he asks Jay, the volunteer who works at the front desk.

"A couple of big ones," Jay tells him. "A lab mix and something with some retriever in him."

The clown has put up signs around the neighborhood. He ran an ad in the local weekly until it got too expensive. One day Jay offered to help him pass out fliers down by the beach. He and Jay did this for about an hour and then Jay asked him if he wanted to go get a margarita.

"It's so hot out," Jay said.

The clown was unimpressed.

"You want to quit just because it's hot out?" the clown asked him.

- - - - - - - -

When the clown gets up this morning he stands at his bay window and stares out at his front yard. His lawn is gnarly and overgrown. It needs to be mowed, but the clown is too tired to deal with it. The city has cited him. His neighbors continue to complain. They yell at the clown whenever he walks to his car.

The clown tries not to respond to any of their taunts, but sometimes he cannot help himself. He yells back at them about how he is letting the grass grow on purpose, how there is a grand plan at work, how he's returning his lawn to native grassland, to the way it was before any of them arrived here.

As the clown stands at the counter and sips his mint tea, the phone rings. He picks it up. This time it's his ex-boyfriend, Reggie.

"Listen," Reggie tells the clown. "I can't help you pay for Grosvent. No matter how much I loved Choco, I just don't have the money."

Grosvent is the private eye that the clown hired last week. Grosvent specializes in missing pets. The clown hired him to go over the case one last time. He is the third pet detective that the clown has retained. The clown has a good feeling about him. Grosvent has a small picture of a Boston Terrier on his business card and he wears a fedora. The clown likes how sad Grosvent's eyes look and how there seems to be some sort of menace behind that sadness.

"Then I guess I'm on the hook for the entire thing," the clown tells Reggie.

The clown does not have the money for Grosvent either. He is a hard-working clown, but there is not enough now that Reggie has moved out.

"Do you really think that Choco is ever going to be found?" Reggie asks him. "Do you honestly still believe that?"

The clown eats stale pretzels from an open bag on the counter.

The clown knows what Reggie thinks. Reggie thinks that a hawk or an eagle snatched Choco up. That might be the case, the clown supposes, but there are also dognappers roaming around the city looking for purebreds to send to puppy farms. Why are dognappers any less likely than a bird of prey? Why were *his* scenarios always so much less likely to Reggie?

"There comes a point when you need to pack it in," Reggie tells him.

The clown does not know which thing Reggie is talking about now. Is he referring to their relationship? Is he only talking about Choco? Is Reggie talking about how everything that they had is now all mashed together and fucked up into one mashed up and fucked together thing?

Sometimes the clown likes to imagine when he gets one of late night breathing calls that it is one of his old boyfriends, one of the ones before Reggie, calling him. That maybe one of them holds a torch for the clown and would like to get together for a nice dinner and some cheek-to-cheek dancing. When he cannot sleep, the clown ticks through the list of men he has slept with. It does not take him long enough, he thinks. He wishes that it took him days, not seconds, to compile a list like this.

The clown conducts his own investigation after he finishes work today. He walks down to the dog park and posts a picture of Choco on the community bulletin board at the co-op. He nails posters onto neighborhood telephone poles. He goes down to the jogging path and pushes fliers into the chests of runners and bikers as they pass. While he is there, Grosvent calls with an update.

"I spoke to your former housekeeper, Allison Shaw," Grosvent says.

The clown has suspected Allison Shaw from the beginning. The clown knows that she was mixed up in this, just not how.

Maybe she unlocked the gate for the dognappers. Maybe she stole Choco for herself. Maybe Allison Shaw was lonely and she stole Choco and brought him to her house to sleep at the foot of her bed.

"Did she finally admit her guilt?" the clown asks.

"She said that she would retain a lawyer if you keep bothering her," he tells the clown.

"That means she's hiding something, right?" the clown asks.

"It probably means that she'll retain a lawyer if you keep bothering her," Grosvent says.

The clown finally drifts off to sleep, but then the phone rings and wakes him. He scrambles for it. He does not want to answer this call, but he cannot take the chance not to pick it up.

"Hello?" he says.

And there is that awful sound again, that sneering screech of metal on metal. Behind it, there is a clicking that sounds like the creaky wheels of an old tape recorder.

"Is this about Choco?" the clown yells.

There is a long sigh on the other end of the phone and then a flat click and the line goes dead.

The clown will not be able to fall asleep now. He knows this. He gets up and walks into the kitchen. He fills up his skull glass with more brandy, drinks it down in one gulp. He leans on the kitchen counter and stares out the window. His lawn is almost knee high now. He watches it bend and flop in the breeze. The city has sent a letter telling him that a crew of men will descend upon his yard at some point in the next few days. A crew will come with weed whips and wood chippers and ride-along mowers and the clown will be charged a high rate for their time.

The clown finds the letter from the city in his pile of unpaid bills. He turns on the burner on his stove and puts the letter over it. He watches the flame slide down the letter and sees the paper char and curl away. His window is open and the smoke from the letter gets sucked out through the screen. The clown closes his eyes and listens to that great sound that long grass makes when the wind weaves through it—*whoosh, whoosh, whoosh.*

KALISPELL

Jacob Ellsworth was finding it difficult to compete with a skywriter for a woman's heart. Especially in Kalispell, Montana, on a windless morning in the spring of 1926 when the sky was vast and blue and his competitor's smoky statement of love would likely hold its sentiment for the entire afternoon.

"Blakely's written something again?" Ellsworth asked the hotel clerk, Mr. Bristol.

Mornings were normally bad for Ellsworth's vertigo, but this one had been particularly unsettling. That morning, Ellsworth's balance was precarious enough that the only way for him to arrive to breakfast was to unceremoniously bump down the front stairs on his ass.

"Indeed," Bristol told him. "And there's a rumor that he's going back up again tonight."

Since Ellsworth's arrival, Mr. Bristol had become an indispensable ally. For a nominal fee, the clerk kept Ellsworth abreast of the yondered overtures of Willem Blakely, made the necessary calls to Dr. McGillicutty for Ellsworth's healing powders, and provided important insight into Miss Jessica Yates's strange and wonderful heart.

"Does this man ever sleep?" Ellsworth asked.

Ellsworth widened his stance, steadied himself on the pane of the bay window. He looked out onto the street at Willem Blakely's biplane, a growling mouth painted on its cutter. Blakely had parked the plane right in front of the bank like it was some brindled mare thirsty for the trough. And if that wasn't bad enough, Blakely leaned on the metallic beast now, holding court with a gaggle of cowpunchers and oil riggers. All of the men kept pointing to the sky and then slapping and reslapping Blakely's broad back.

Ellsworth closed his eyes. Without his healing powders, his body felt like a small boat fighting a horrible squall—up then down, waves and swells, again and again. He went down to a knee, overcome.

"Summon Dr. McGillicutty," he told Bristol.

Even though he was unable to stand for extended periods of time, Ellsworth still had certain merits. His most recent invention—a candlewick that burned twice as long as the industry standard—had brought him considerable fame within the candlewicking and wax-molding worlds. And while he was not particularly handsome, Ellsworth wasn't unseemly either. He sported a well-groomed beard. He smoked a good-smelling pipe. He used his monocle only when it was absolutely necessary.

Even with these attributes, Ellsworth could not escape the uneasy feeling in the pit of his barrel chest that in this particular instance, competing with the square-jawed Mr. Blakely, he was far out of his league.

It was obvious. Obvious to the entire town of Kalispell, who regarded Ellsworth as a dizzy interloper. Obvious to Blakely, the hometown war hero who'd shot down seventeen enemy planes in the Great War. But most of all, it was obvious to Ellsworth. Even though he told himself otherwise, he could not sugarcoat what he saw in the mirror each morning—that he was a stout man, that he was a man prone to mucus, that he was a man whose eyes were perpetually set in a wincing squint.

And yet, and yet, and yet. For some strange reason, these things did not seem off-putting to Miss Jessica Yates. Just that afternoon at the bank—her hair curled into dropping ringlets, her ample bust fighting gravity like a wall shelf—Miss Yates was as encouraging to Ellsworth as she'd ever been.

"Sit down right here," she told him, pulling a chair close enough for him to smell the lemon verbena dotted behind her ears.

"Will you call upon me tonight?" she asked.

This would be the third time that Ellsworth had called upon her that week. While Blakely filled the sky with words of his undying love for Miss Yates, Ellsworth spent quiet hours with his feet firmly planted on the floorboards of her living room.

"I'll be by at seven," Ellsworth said. "And I'll bring more of Mr. Bristol's ragtime records."

Miss Yates looked up from her ledger and smiled at him—she had good teeth. Right then, Ellsworth thought about her using them to bite him. Right on his chest, hard, right through his skin; suddenly he wanted her to take a big chunk out of his body, take it and never give it back.

"That would be lovely," she told him. "You have so much more to tell me about New York."

City life certainly held Miss Yates's fascination. Each night Ellsworth sat on her sofa she prodded him for stories—about the nightlife, about plays and movies that he'd seen, about the famous people he knew.

Ellsworth had already recounted the time he'd seen Fatty Arbuckle on the Upper West Side. This was before all of Fatty's troubles, before his ruinous trial—Fatty dressed like a dandy, standing at a deli counter ordering sandwiches and potato salad, a woman on each of his elbows.

"What was he like?" she'd asked Ellsworth.

"He was fat," Ellsworth told her. "Just like you'd think."

Miss Yates had a well-worn magazine that showed beauty portraits of dewy-eyed starlets dressed in their finery, and whenever the conversation lagged with Ellsworth, she opened it and carefully turned the pages, telling Ellsworth how much she'd already missed by living in Kalispell.

"The only stage we have here is the one in the whorehouse," she told him. "I mean, if you haven't realized it yet, this town's completely bereft of cultural goings-on."

Even though Ellsworth was growing somewhat weary with her interest in big cities, he did not let on. While Miss Yates was certainly fetching, there was something else, something much more important, that drew Ellsworth to her. Whenever he was around her, the vertigo that he had mysteriously caught traveling back to the east from San Francisco, the ass-over-teakettle dizziness that had forced him off the train in Kalispell to recuperate, it all slid away. When Miss Yates was near him, Ellsworth's world rotated back into balance, the overwhelming pressure in his ears leaked away, there was no longer a need for the ballast of McGillicutty's healing powder. The horizon was finally, for Ellsworth, where the horizon was supposed to be.

"Come back with me," he begged her once again. "And I'll show you all of it."

But then, but then, but then. When he was not in the presence of Miss Yates, Ellsworth spent much of his time alone in his hotel room, lying on the lumpy bed, staring up at the cobwebbed ceiling. This dire view, coupled with the ponderous thoughts that bumped to and fro in his roiling head, made it hard for Ellsworth not to question his place in Miss Yates's heart.

One thing that helped buoy Ellsworth during these periods of doubt was Mr. Bristol. Bristol came to his room toting a bottle of bourbon, sat in the overstuffed chair by the bed, and gossiped about Blakely's bona fides.

"He caught syphilis when he was a flyboy in the war," Bristol told him. "And he was married once previous."

Back east, Ellsworth would have thought Bristol a classless toady, would not have sipped bourbon with the man, but here in this forsaken town, Ellsworth was glad for the bottle, glad for the bonhomie.

"And I heard there's a newborn three counties over," Bristol continued. "A jilted lover that goes along with the kid."

Ellsworth hoped these rumors Bristol spouted about Blakely were God's honest, but who knew? Ellsworth paid Bristol and he couldn't help but wonder whether the statements about Blakely weren't born out of commerce. He took another pull from the bourbon, passed the bottle back to Bristol.

"What it boils down to," Bristol told him, "is that Miss Yates sees the bad in him and the good in you. That's all you need to know."

Later that day, after Bristol had left him, Ellsworth attempted to convince himself of Bristol's words, but he could not. From the outset, he'd wondered if he was being used, if he was an actor in some demented play that Miss Yates had authored to simply make Blakely crazy with jealousy.

The worst part of all, something Ellsworth could surely see even without his monocle, something there was no way for him to dismiss, was that Blakely and Miss Yates made a fine couple. Both of their faces were symmetrical and finely featured and their bodies looked cut from the same sculptor's blade. They fit together.

Ellsworth and Miss Yates? His only hope was a small one— he'd seen plenty of pretty women in New York overlook a man's physical defects for a thick pocketbook.

Lying on his bed now, Ellsworth dug into the breast pocket of his shirt. He pulled out his packet of McGillicutty's healing powder. Instead of brewing it into a tea as the doctor had suggested, Ellsworth had taken to snorting it directly. He poured a bit onto his knuckle and then pushed it up into his nostril. His eyes watered and he felt the chalky resolve in his throat and then he felt the powder hit his blood stream. A chill went up his spine. He teetered upward, made his way over to his valise. He opened it, took out one of the prototype candles he'd shown the wax manufacturers in San Francisco. He struck a match, lit it.

In the candlelight, standing in front of the mirror, Ellsworth sucked in his gut and then buttoned his vest. He yanked his suspenders over his shoulders. He took a deep breath, slid on his tweed jacket.

On his walk to Miss Yates's that evening, Ellsworth had the dubious pleasure of watching Blakely write a new message of love in the night sky. By now Blakely's flights had turned into a community activity, like a threshing bee or fireworks on the 4th, everyone coming out of their houses and sitting on blankets by the riverbed. Ellsworth sauntered down Main Street as Blakely's plane dipped and rose. "Jess," the townspeople said in unison. Then, "Jess will you." Then "Jess will you ever." Finally, the town of Kalispell chanted Blakely's contrailed query out loud like a Greek chorus— "Jess," they yelled, "will you ever be mine?"

As Ellsworth walked, the pressure in his ears steadily increased and his legs became shaky. About a block away from Miss Yates's, he could not continue. He staggered over to the curb and collapsed. He sat down just in time to watch Blakely dot the question mark by dropping straight down toward the Earth and then pulling his smoke lever for just a second. A small round puff, like it had come from Ellsworth's pipe. It was so impressive, the precise dotting of that question mark, that Ellsworth forgot who was flying the plane, forgot where he was, forgot that he was supposed to hate Willem Blakely. Ellsworth was caught up in the artistry of the moment and before he noticed what he was doing, before his brain could stop his hands, he began to clap.

Outside Miss Yates's door, Ellsworth steadied himself with another knuckle's worth of McGillicutty's powder. He wiped his nose on his sleeve and knocked. When the door swung open, the first thing Ellsworth noticed were Miss Yates's cheeks. They were rosier than normal, full of a rageful fire. She spun away from him without a word, walked to her decanter of speakeasy scotch, poured three fingers into a lowball, brought it to her lips and swallowed.

"No one owns me," she said, walking to the window. "No one pressures me into anything."

Ellsworth was still holding Bristol's ragtime records under his arm, and he stood and watched Miss Yates fume. She was wearing a red dress and had her hair pulled back in a bun. She stood in front of the window, shaking her head back and forth.

"No one could ever own you," he assured her. "That would be impossible."

Miss Yates stayed at the window while Ellsworth moved to the phonograph. He pulled a record from the sleeve, set it down. He wound the player and he dropped the needle and the sound of a jaunty piano filled the room. Miss Yates had sung for him the last time he was here, extremely well, in fact, sung in a lilting soprano along with one of the Joplin records he'd brought. After she'd finished the song, it seemed to Ellsworth like there was maybe nothing Miss Yates couldn't do—that her life might be wasted by anyone she was with, that maybe there wasn't anyone in this world who could make her truly happy.

"This town," she said shaking her head. "As if their carrying on is going to make my heart overflow with love."

Miss Yates sat down next to him on the couch then and took his hand in hers. Ellsworth had thought he would be prepared for something like this, for such a small amount of affection, a concrete sign of her interest, but he was not. He realized then that Miss Yates's touch, no matter how chaste, made him dizzy again, but in a completely different way, a way he would choose no matter the cost.

"Come back east with me," he said again.

Miss Yates slid her hand from his fingers. She walked back to the window, stood there looking out. She turned back to Ellsworth, set her gaze on him.

"Fine," she told him. "I will."

Ellsworth suspected that Blakely was drunk that next morning when he went up in his biplane. He watched as Blakely filled the sky with a white smoky mess, a child's angry scribble.

"She must have told him," Bristol said as he loaded Ellsworth's bags into the surrey. "She must have told him what's what."

Ellsworth had to admit that Bristol had been a godsend that morning. He'd coordinated the sleeping car with the train steward, procured a rig to take them to the platform, cabled Ellsworth's people in New York about the couple's impending arrival.

"She must have," Ellsworth nodded.

Looking up at the sky, Ellsworth suddenly felt for Blakely, understood that his competitor's heartache might well have been his own. At the same time, Ellsworth's empathy was a small undercurrent in the buoyancy that filled his heart. He was brimming, hadn't needed a grain of McGillicutty's powder that entire morning. His legs felt as good as they had in weeks, vigorous and sturdy.

He and Bristol drove the surrey over to Miss Yates's, gathered up her bags. She was wearing a yellow dress and a large brimmed sunhat, her braided hair snaking down her spine.

"Are you ready, my darling?" Ellsworth asked.

"I've been ready for this my entire life," she told him.

The next afternoon, when the train arrived in Chicago, Miss Yates would tell Ellsworth that she needed some fresh air. She would kiss him on the cheek and leave their sleeping compartment. Ellsworth would watch from the train window as she sashayed down the platform and disappeared into the bustling crowd.

Ellsworth would not notice that his wallet was missing until the train whistle blew. He would notice a few minutes later that his pocket watch was gone. He would depart the train and spend the next two weeks searching the city for Miss Yates, but he would never see her again.

Now, though, as they made their way to the station in Kalispell, her gloved hand sat like a white pearl in Ellsworth's palm. He wrapped his fingers around it, squeezed. Miss Yates looked up at him and smiled.

"Those teeth," Ellsworth thought to himself, "those beautiful teeth."

VESSELS

A man recently brought me this metal briefcase. He set it down on the bar near where I sat. Somehow he knew where to find me. He called me by my given name, Ronald. It was getting cold outside, but he was really sweating, this man, these little rivers of water running down his forehead.

"This was your father's," he said, pushing the case toward me. "I worked with him. I think he'd want you to have it."

I hadn't talked to my father in a long while. Years. My mother had died a long time ago. Last I heard my father was traveling around Ohio selling aluminum siding.

I picked up the metal case. I could tell the handle on it had melted a little, but then had cooled down. It had this drippy plastic look that you see sometimes when things get too hot.

"There was a fire," the man told me. "At his motel."

The man proceeded to tell me that someone had fallen asleep smoking in the roadside motel that my father was staying in. This was outside Akron, he said. His briefcase was the only thing left over from his room. It was one of the only things out of the entire place that had made it, he said.

The man told me he was driving through here on business, so he thought he'd bring it along and give it to me.

"Heat like that—everything usually melts," he told me. He pointed at the briefcase. "This made it through, though."

The man looked really thirsty, so I got Geno the bartender to put down his tattoo magazine and bring us some drinks.

"Are you okay?" I asked the man. With all the sweat, he wasn't looking so healthy.

"I need to show you something," he said.

We walked outside to his car and he popped open the trunk. My eyes took a second to focus, but when they did, I couldn't believe what I saw—there were three little girls in there, sleeping. There was a bigger one and then the other two got progressively smaller, like Russian stacking dolls.

"They're still my kids," he told me. "Even if their mother doesn't think so."

I kept on looking in that trunk. It was huge! The kids had pillows and blankets and they looked really comfortable. I noticed that the man had drilled some holes in the trunk for ventilation. I wondered why I hadn't thought of doing something like this to a car.

"Wow," I told him.

He shut the trunk gently and we walked back into the bar. He was sweating less now and had calmed down some. After a bit, he pointed at my father's briefcase.

"Aren't you going to look at what's inside?" he asked.

I didn't think that there would be anything important inside, but I popped the latch on the case and slid it open. There were some invoices written out in my father's hand, a pack of cigarettes, some siding brochures.

"I was hoping for gold bricks," I said. "But no such luck."

The man and I sat silently watching the football game on the TV above the bar. After a while he stood up to go.

"Hey," I said. "Can I see them once last time?"

He nodded and we walked out to his car and he opened the trunk. The girls were still in there, all three of them, safe and asleep, same as before.

"Great," I told him. "Thank you for doing that."

The man slowly closed the trunk. We shook hands. Then he got in his car and drove off down the street. I watched his taillights trail away from me. After a little bit, he put on his blinker, turned the corner and was gone.

THE DEADSITTER

I get paid eight dollars an hour to pretend I am Vincent, Mrs. Ramon's dead son. I do this on Saturdays from noon to four. I walk next door to Mrs. Ramon's house and then I go down to Vincent's old room and change into the outfit lying on his old bed. I wet a comb and part my hair over to the right. When I walk upstairs, there is a bowl of orange sherbet waiting for me on the dining room table. I am supposed to take the spoon and eat the orange sherbet like it is my favorite thing.

Sometimes when I go to Mrs. Ramon's house, Vincent gets a bad report card and there is no bowl of sherbet on the table. When that happens I sit patiently and listen to Mrs. Ramon lecture me about how important education is for my future. I nod my head and try to look guilty. I make a solemn promise to her that from now on, I will take World Geography much more seriously.

Sometimes it is Vincent's birthday and there is a cake shaped like a racecar and a new ten-speed bike in the driveway and I have to pretend that a car-shaped cake and a new ten-speed are both very exciting, that these are the things that I want most in the entire world.

Mrs. Ramon is pretty and usually she smells good. It is not really her that I do not like. It is mostly that I am sick of Vincent's green tennis shoes that are two sizes too small, that I am sick of wearing that acid washed jean jacket with a huge butterfly embroidered on the back, that I am sick of acting like a dead kid when I, Steve Keppler, am very much alive.

"I'm quitting," I tell my family at dinner tonight. "It is getting way too creepy over there. I am done."

"You keep going over there until she tells you not to," my brother Grant says. "She's a nice lady and hell if you are going to disappoint her."

Grant was Vincent before I was Vincent. When Grant got too big for the clothes, he brought me over there and walked me through everything. Our older brother Jake did the same thing with Grant a couple of years before that. Jake actually knew the real Vincent, who was only a couple years ahead of him in school. If it was only Grant telling me to continue I would not care, but my parents are on board too. They think that working for Mrs. Ramon teaches me empathy, that pretending to be a dead kid makes me appreciate how lucky I am to be alive.

"You're just going to leave her in a lurch?" my father asks me as he pushes a bowl of mashed potatoes across the table to my mother. "She's counting on you and you're just going to turn your back?"

I am the youngest child and there isn't anyone else in my family to send. Vincent died when he was nine years old, but I am turning thirteen next week. The legs of Vincent's jeans end halfway up my calf. A couple of hairs have sprouted on my balls and fuck if I am going over there one more goddamn Saturday.

"What if I find someone else?" I ask them. "What then?"

- - - - - - -

At recess on Monday, I corner a smallish fifth grader named Todd Billups. I ask him if he wants to make some money.

"How?" he asks.

"You've got to pretend you're a dead kid," I say.

"Just lay there?" he says. "In one of those creepy kid coffins?"

"You've got to do stuff," I tell him. "You are playing a dead kid who's alive."

"I'd be playing a kid who comes back from the dead?" he says. "Like a kid zombie?"

"No," I explain. "You're pretending like you're the dead kid, but that you never died."

"How the hell does that work?" he asks.

Sometimes I ask myself this question. Sometimes I wonder how this works in Mrs. Ramon's head. What does she do for the rest of the week? Does she pretend that Vincent is at church camp or boarding school? That he's off visiting relatives?

"You go there and you put on his clothes and then you talk to the dead kid's mom," I tell Todd. "You do whatever the lady wants you to do and then you go home. It's easy."

Todd still looks reluctant, so I remind him about the money.

"You can buy a lot of shit with that money," I say. "A lot of shit."

This is a true statement, but what I fail to mention to Todd is what the money feels like when you spend it. I do not tell Todd that anything you buy with this money has a strange feeling attached to it. For instance that when you look down at your new pair of shoes the only thing you think is: death, death, death.

"Do you want to try it out on Saturday?" I ask.

Todd rides his bike over to my house on Saturday morning and we walk over to Mrs. Ramon's. I bring Todd downstairs to Vincent's room and point to the clothes on the bed.

"You'll need to put these on," I say.

Todd walks over and studies the clothes. He picks up the green shoes and then drops them back onto the floor. He's a short kid and unless he gets a big growth spurt he can do this job for a long time.

"I'm not wearing any of this," he tells me.

"It's part of the job," I tell him. "It's what you signed up for."

Todd slides on the jean jacket, pops the collar on it so it's up near his ears. He sticks his hands out and front of him and starts to moan.

"And I already told you—no zombies."

Todd doesn't listen to me and continues to moan. He picks up Vincent's thin gray t-shirt that has a picture of a bull's-eye on it with the words "Hot Shot" underneath. I can tell that now that he is having his doubts.

"I'll wear the jean jacket," he says. "But not any of the other stuff."

"You have to wear the whole outfit or you don't get the money," I tell him. "That's the deal."

"Then there's no deal," he says, peeling off the jacket and starting toward the door.

I know that I should let Todd go. I know that I should find someone else who can follow these simple rules, some poor kid who really needs the money, but I am not sure that there are many people like that in the world.

Maybe Todd can make it work wearing only the jean jacket, I think. Maybe Mrs. Ramon is so whacked out that she only needs a warm body sitting next to her. Maybe she won't even realize what he's wearing.

"Fine, fine," I say. "We can try it your way."

I hear Todd up above me, tromping across the living room floor.

I want to leave now and be done with this forever, but I decide to wait and make sure it goes okay. I lie down on Vincent's bed and pick up an old magazine from the bedside table. I page through it, look at these goofy-haired teen stars of yesterday. They are nearly as old as my parents now. Some of them are probably older.

After about five minutes, I hear a low-pitched zombie moan coming from upstairs. Then I hear Mrs. Ramon scream. After that Todd runs back downstairs. He wads up the jean jacket and throws it at me.

"I tried," he tells me, "but I guess she just wasn't buying it."

After Todd leaves, I sit on the bed and listen to Mrs. Ramon wail. Her sobs are high-pitched, sort of like when a vacuum cleaner throws a belt, part whirring and part flapping. It is an awful noise, something that I want to make stop immediately. I put on the jean jacket and smash my feet into those damn shoes. I walk upstairs and sit down on the couch next to her. She does not say anything to me for about ten minutes. I listen to the buzzing of her refrigerator. I hear a delivery truck bump down our street. Finally, I cannot take the silence any longer.

"How about we look at a photo album?" I say.

This is the absolute last thing I want to do, but I go over to the hutch and I pull out a large brown picture album with the words "Family Memories" on it. I open it up and I turn the pages. I ask Mrs. Ramon questions about the people in the pictures. After a bit, she stops crying.

"That is your Great Uncle Joshua," she tells me, pointing to a picture of a man with a huge belly who is tending a grill.

While we are sitting there looking at these pictures, I can't help but stare outside. It's a beautiful afternoon and when I look out the window I can see my father and brother throwing a football in our yard.

While I am looking outside, I see Mr. Ramon pull up the driveway. Mr. Ramon does not live with Mrs. Ramon any more.

He lives in a condo across town. He comes over once a week to mow the lawn and bring Mrs. Ramon groceries. He wants no part of this Vincent nonsense either. Whenever I see him, he will not even look my way. Why am I on the hook for this, I think as I sit here, how does deadsitting for Mrs. Ramon fall to me?

"People say you look like Uncle Joshua," Mrs. Ramon says.

I study the picture of Uncle Joshua. He doesn't look anything like me. It's not even close. I've got dark curly hair and brown eyes and Uncle Joshua has white blond hair and ruddy skin. Screw this.

"Is Great Uncle Joshua dead?" I ask Mrs. Ramon.

"Yes," Mrs. Ramon tells me. "He passed away a few years ago."

I point to another person, this time a woman standing next to Uncle Joshua.

"What about that lady?" I say.

"Your Great Aunt Eunice?" Mrs. Ramon asks.

"Sure," I say. "What about her? Is she dead?"

"Yes," she says. "She passed away just after Uncle Joshua."

We page through the album. Now though, instead of only looking at the pictures, I point at every person in each picture and ask Mrs. Ramon if they are dead.

"What about that lady holding the cigarette?" I ask. "How did she die?"

For a while, Mrs. Ramon answers my questions. Slowly, though, she catches on to what I am doing. When she does she stands up and goes into the bathroom. Through the door, I hear her sobbing.

"Listen," I say to her. "I don't think I can do this anymore. I need to be finished. Okay?"

"Vincent?" she says.

"My name is not Vincent," I tell her. "You know that."

The door flies open and Mrs. Ramon stares at me with huge, scared eyes. Her mascara has run in black rivers down into the neck of her blouse.

"Vincent," she tells me, "you need to stop playing these games right this instant."

"How was the replacement?" my mother asks me at dinner.

"Not good," I say. "He left after five minutes."

"You'll find another one," my father says.

"Sure I will," I say.

"It'll be easy," Grant says.

I decide that there is only one way out of this and so I call up Todd again.

"What now?" he asks.

"I've been thinking this over," I tell him. "And I've decided that you need to kill me next Saturday."

"For real dead?" he says.

"Not for real dead," I say. "It just needs to look for real."

"How are you going to do it?" he asks.

"Stabbing," I say. "I looked on the Internet and I can make it look real."

"Can I dress up like a zombie?" he asks me.

"I don't see why not," I say.

We plan the specifics the next day at recess. I will tape two baggies full of corn syrup to my chest. At precisely 12:30 pm Todd will run inside the house and stab these bags with a fork. I will scream very loudly and the blood will spurt out of my chest. I will run outside and die very dramatically on Mrs. Ramon's front lawn.

Todd shakes his head back and forth.

"This plan is stupid," he says.

"It doesn't matter," I say. "It just has to work."

- - - - - - - -

On Saturday I get up early and mix up the two baggies of red corn syrup and go over to Mrs. Ramon's house. I go down into Vincent's old room. I slide into his pants. I tape the baggies to my chest and put on his shirt over them. I lace up his shoes and I slip on his jean jacket and walk upstairs. Every time I move there is a loud sloshing sound.

"Hello?" I say. "Mom?"

All the lights in the house are off. There is no bowl of orange sherbet sitting on the kitchen table. I hear the air conditioning kick on. I am near a vent and the cool air travels up my pant leg.

"Hello?" I yell out again.

I hear a noise in the bedroom and I walk down the hall. I push open the door. The room is dark, but I can see that Mrs. Ramon is lying on the bed. She is under the covers, her body turned away from me.

"I didn't know if you were coming back," she says.

The way these words come out of her mouth makes it seem like she's in great pain, like each word that travels to her tongue is a struggle to push out of her mouth and into the air.

"I'm here," I say.

Mrs. Ramon inhales deeply. She sits and puts her feet on the floor. I shift my feet and the liquid in the baggies move across my chest.

"So you are," she says. She gets up from the bed and makes her way into the kitchen. She goes into the freezer and scoops out some sherbet into a bowl and sets it out in front of me. She sits down across the table.

"Eat," she says.

I spoon the sherbet into my mouth.

"How is it?" she asks.

"It is the same as always," I say.

"That's good," she says. "Right?"

"Sure," I say. "That's good."

When I finish, I get up and bring my bowl to the sink and rinse it out.

When I turn around, Mrs. Ramon is standing right behind me. She is much too close. I can smell her perfume, something with lemon. An eyelash has fallen from her eye and is resting on her cheek.

"Is everything okay?" I ask.

Mrs. Ramon does not answer me. Instead, she pulls me in for a hug. She takes my head and presses it into her chest. I am having trouble breathing, but she holds me close for a long time and when she lets me go, she grabs my shoulders with both of her hands. Hard.

"Mrs. Ramon," I say. "You are hurting me."

Her eyes are somewhere else, looking past or through me, I can't tell which. She loosens her grip and her hands fall to her sides.

"I'm sorry," she says.

"It's okay," I tell her.

She nods and then turns away from me. She walks back down the hall to her bedroom and closes the door behind her.

I stand at the kitchen sink. I hear a branch from a nearby tree scrape against the roof, back and forth in the wind.

I am still standing there when the front door opens and Todd comes inside. He is wearing tattered jeans and a torn t-shirt. He has painted his face with gray makeup. There is a scar running over the bridge of his nose and down his cheek.

"Hold on," I tell him. "We don't have to do it now."

Todd lurches up the stairs and across the living room. There is stiffness in his limbs and his feet drag across on the carpet.

"Todd," I yell, "It's okay now."

He is moaning so loudly that he cannot hear me. A line of drool slides from the corner of his mouth. I wave my hands in front of my face, try to get him to stop. He does not stop. He drags himself toward me, slowly, patiently, like this is the only thing in the world that matters.

INVENTORY

Our baby swallowed a ninja star and then it swallowed a Bakelite button. It seemed fine. Breathing and everything. We checked. We are fine parents.

We weren't too upset about the button, but the ninja star was one of my husband's favorites, really light and made from this tungsten polymer that was said to be "space-age." He used it in the league that he was in on Thursdays nights.

"I'll never ever find another one like that again," he told me privately.

The same thing happened with our toenail clippers.

One night, I found the baby (who knows how babies do this) standing on top of our bathroom sink, rifling through the medicine cabinet.

"The nail clippers are gone," my husband told me after taking stock. "They were right here on this shelf and now they are not."

"Maybe you left them downstairs," I offered. "Maybe you're mistaken. Maybe you left them somewhere where you forgot. Maybe you were the one."

My husband had just gotten out of bed and his hair was all matted down. It looked like when a helicopter comes down suddenly in high grass, pushed out in spots, flattened down in others.

"Whose side are you on here?" he asked me.

"No one's," I told him. "And everyone's."

Soon, my husband and the baby were eyeing each other in a manner I did not like. You see it all the time nowadays, this raising of eyebrows, a puffing out of chests, hands flexing from open to closed.

One night, my husband searched the baby's bassinet.

"This is a random search," he told the baby. "It could occur at any time. That's what random means, okay?"

The baby took its revenge for the search by swallowing my husband's wristwatch.

"It's on," my husband told our marriage counselor. "That was an heirloom. Handed down from generation to generation. Game fucking on."

"Maybe the baby will pass all this stuff," I offered.

Pass it? That was one thing we knew the baby would *not* do. Things disappeared inside this baby, pellets of rock salt, packs of post-it notes, diamond solitaire necklaces, whatever. Gone. Finito. Seeya.

Sometimes I put my head right up to the baby's stomach, my ears to its skin, listened to its innards to see if I could hear something moving along.

Passing these things?

"Good one," my husband said. "Hardy-har."

- - - - - - - -

Finally, I started leaving things out for the baby to swallow. A puzzle piece with no matching puzzle. A broken half of a letter opener. A combination lock to which we'd forgotten the combination.

I put these things in plain view.

I left out sheets of paper too. Words written on them in big black marker. Phrases like "Crying Over Nothing." Phrases like "Taking All This For Granted."

I motioned to the baby.

"Here," I said.

I gave the baby one of those sudden hey, hey over here moves you give with your hands when you think someone can help.

One morning, I woke up to find my hand duct taped to my husband's hand, this big silver cocoon running up to both our elbows like a shiny cast.

I knew right away.

No note, no word of thanks, not one iota of goodwill for the time that we'd put in. Just the duct tape around our arms.

"Call everyone we know," I said to my husband.

He picked up the phone in his free hand, held it out to me. With my free hand, I dialed. After I punched in the numbers, he held the phone up to his ear.

"Hello," he said to our people, "the baby's gone."

"Not our fault," I called from the background.

"Not our fault," he repeated.

Later that night, after we'd broken the news to everyone, we got up and walked around the house. Looked at what was left.

Garlic press, we said. Recordable DVD. Alarm clock.

We touched these things, ran our free hands over them.

After a while, we found a notebook.

This was a lucky thing.

In it, we started to take inventory.

All it boiled down to was this: one person telling the other one what they saw, then the other person, the one with the pen and the free hand, writing it all down.

THE BARNACLE

My brother's girlfriend came home with a barnacle stuck to her butt cheek.

"Rory," Jill said to me, pointing to her butt. "It happened again."

Jill was my age. My brother, Phillip, was older. We all lived together in Phillip's place across the highway from the ocean.

"Again?" I said.

Jill said she'd fallen asleep at the beach and then it was there under her bikini bottom, the barnacle, all misshapen and hard and about the size of a fist.

Jill was at the beach getting tan for a bikini contest. She'd won one at a local hot rod show, which qualified her for the state meet. The state meet was tomorrow. Jill was taking it all serious, even though everyone kept telling her she wasn't curvy enough to win.

"*Again*," she said to me.

Yes, this had happened before. One other time. Right when Jill had started going out with Phillip. Right at the beginning, when everything was still new and exciting for them. It was all a joke then. Something funny they told people at their beach parties.

A barnacle.

Can you believe it?

I was still in broadcasting school the first time it happened. I had just broken up with Corrine. I was ready to quit everything. Corrine was telling me that she didn't love me anymore, that we weren't meant to be together. Everyone else was telling me that my voice was too nasally, that I'd never make it in radio.

Not even in public radio, my teachers said.

I was in my dorm room when I got Phillip's phone call about the first barnacle. We hardly ever talked on the phone. The only other time he'd called me at school he'd told me that our mother had died. I was sitting there, waiting for him to tell me some other horrible news, but instead he told me about Jill.

"Other than the barnacle, she's great," Phillip said. "I can't keep my hands off her."

Now though, two times, it was way less funny, maybe even ominous. Maybe there was something about Jill that just attracted things from the briny deep.

Last time it was on her calf. She'd forgotten about high tide that time too, woke up to water skidding up her legs. This one on her butt cheek was way bigger. It looked medieval, looked like it had seen a lot of shit in its day.

"Just get the damn salt," Jill told me. "I can feel it really attaching itself, thinking this is its new home."

Salt worked the last time. Even though Jill told Phillip that was what you did for leeches, not barnacles, for some reason it worked, the barnacle slid right off her leg.

I walked into the pantry now, lifted up the salt container. It was empty.

"We're out," I yelled back to her.

- - - - - - - -

We lived in a tiny house across the highway from the ocean. You could yell anywhere in there and be heard from anywhere else. And that is what Jill and I usually did. In different rooms, yelling through the walls—back and forth at each other. We weren't much on politeness or decency. Jill and I battled and yes, sometimes things escalated. Once she stuck a fork into my shoulder. I still had the scar—the three tine marks. It looked like some messed-up vampire had bitten me.

The reasons I didn't like Jill were numerous, but the worst thing Jill had done was to sort of resemble Corrine. I'll admit that ultimately they didn't look all that much alike, but sometimes looking at her lounging on the couch, her blond hair in braids, the freckles that lightly dotted her cheeks—it dug up all the bad feelings between Corrine and me. The only way I knew how to deal with these feelings was to toss some ill will her way.

Usually Phillip let the jawing between Jill and me play out, like it was a rite of passage that we needed to work through to become a family. When it escalated into something more, when we stood up and starting moving at each other, Phillip planted himself between us, his arms extended and unmovable, his hands ready for action.

"Settle the hell down," he'd tell us.

My brother towered over both of us. He'd played defensive tackle at San Diego State and had a weight room set up in the garage to stay ripped. There had been a tryout a few years back for some Arena league, then one in Europe, but they all told him he wasn't fast enough to make it in the pros.

"Let's take a walk down to where it all started," Phillip would say to us, "calm ourselves down."

He'd lead us down the dirt path to the ocean. The path wasn't anything really, just a trail that surfers had worn down over time. There was some sagebrush to grab onto so you didn't fall.

"This can work," he offered, putting his arms around both of us and squeezing us together. "I like both of you, so both of you can like each other, right?"

Once we got down to the ocean, Phillip waxed philosophical. Lately he had been watching a lot of documentaries about evolutionary sea life on the Discovery Channel. He'd just read this biography on Jacques Cousteau.

"Shit crawled out of there," he'd tell us as he pointed at the grey ocean water. "Shit that became you and me."

Here's what I wanted to tell Phillip right now as I looked at the barnacle: "Shit's crawling out of there again, bro. Shit that ended up on your girlfriend's ass."

"I have a crowbar in my car," I told Jill. "Just a couple pulls and you'd be back to normal."

She was lying on the couch, her face buried in throw pillows. She reared up into a yoga pose, legs on the ground, head arching to the ceiling. She was flexible enough for it; she was always exercising in front of the TV, throwing her leg behind her head or some other nonsense.

"Flexibility is one of the key components to longevity," she'd told me yesterday.

"Not stretching makes me not hurt," I responded.

All this stuff she did was for that bikini contest—the videos, running the beach every morning, getting her nails done at the mall, reading women's magazines—prep for this singular moment when she shimmied down the runway and shook her hips.

"I have to be super-prepared," she told me. "People only have a second to decide if they are going to *woo-hoo* for me. Just one second."

It was the same thing with radio. People had only a second

or two to decide whether or not they liked your voice. If they didn't, if they thought you were annoying, if they thought you talked too much, they switched the station. The consensus was that when people heard me talking to them on the radio, they would immediately be reaching for their dials.

"I'll wait for the salt," she said. "Pick some up when you get Scratch and Dent."

That was her pet name for Phillip.

Scratch and Dent.

Like I said, he was older.

I drove downtown to pick up Phillip. He worked as a phlebotomist at this blood bank—had a *career* as a phlebotomist, he emphasized. He'd taken the job after he quit playing football.

"I needed a life skill," he repeated ad nauseam. "Not a pipe dream."

As I drove downtown the sun was setting, cutting the smog into this wicked spectrum, reds and oranges and burnt umbers, all fighting to backlight the city skyline.

Lately, Phillip had been bugging me about my future. Both of our parents had been dead for a few years and he seemed to think he needed to guide me along the career path. I thought that I had been on a good path, with Corrine, with broadcasting school, but then everything got derailed. Now I didn't want to hear about it.

"You can put up with a lot of no's if you love something," he told me. "That's the thing. If you love something, you can sit there and hope forever."

I knew what he was saying, but I was wired in the exact opposite way. Once someone told me no, once someone got in my grill and said I didn't have what it took, I backed the hell off. Right away, no problem. I'd gotten way too sick of hearing the word "no."

Phillip was waiting outside the clinic when I pulled up. He was still dressed in his scrubs. He hopped in the truck and then immediately started telling me a story. I tried to tell him about Jill and the barnacle, but he wouldn't let me get in a word edgewise.

"You should have seen this lady today—I couldn't find a decent vein on her whole fucking body," he said.

He had these stories, you know? He was so much older than both Jill and me and he showed us things about the world we wouldn't have seen otherwise. Maybe it was perspective, maybe experience, maybe both, but I looked at him for what was going to happen to me down the line, how I was going to age, some sort of clue about the future.

"Then I hit the mother lode," he said. "Lady shot out blood like a stuck pig. All over the exam room walls. Totally effed up."

Usually, my brother wasn't an asshole; he worried about what kind of job he did with his clients. That's what he called them, "clients." Like he was selling them something valuable, not poking them in the arm and watching their blood fill up a plastic bag.

I caught a whiff of his breath. "Are you drunk?" I asked him.

"No way," he said. "Never."

He waited a few seconds, then laughed.

"Wasted," he said.

I drove off toward home. Traffic was horrible; we got stuck behind a jackknifed truck and sat for twenty minutes without moving an inch. My brother kept nodding off and then shaking himself back awake. I wasn't going to ask him what happened, why he was drunk. I'd let him tell me when he was good and ready.

"I got canned," he said, breaking the silence. "Staffing cuts. I've been at the bar since noon."

He unzipped his backpack and pulled out a beer. He spun the top off, flicked the cap out the window. I was going to say something about the cops, the open bottle, the littering, but I held back.

"I thought that I was going to do that job for a long time," he said.

I looked over at my brother in the passenger seat. He was hunched over, his arms were wrapped around his legs, his chin was resting on his knees. He was smushed together into this tiny package, sipping his bottle of beer.

"Screw them," I said. "You are way too good for their asses."

I thought this was a particularly positive thing to say, something that would reassure my brother that I was on his side, but he didn't take it that way. He waved me off.

"Don't even start with that crap," he said.

Traffic started moving again. We drove about ten feet and then stopped again.

"Jill's got another barnacle," I told him. "This one's on her ass."

He sat there a minute, let it wash over him. He had talked to me lately about marrying her. He'd been saving up for a ring. I wondered if this would change any of that. That if in his eyes this made her unmarriable.

"Christ," he said. "Again?"

When we got home Jill was lying face down on the couch, moaning.

"I'm not going to urgent care," she told us. "No way. I don't want to explain this. I'll be in that book of urban legends—the mouse up the guy's ass, the vacuum cleaner stuck on the guy's dick. No matter what you say happened, they don't believe you."

Phillip went over and gently kissed her on the forehead. He slid her bikini out of the way and took a look at the barnacle. All of his anger about losing his job seemed to have lifted and I could tell that all he was concerned about now was Jill's welfare.

"Wow," he said. "Big one."

He took the container of salt out of the grocery bag and

opened it. He moved Jill's bikini out of the way, poured a big pile of salt onto the barnacle.

"Now we wait," he told us.

I set the timer on the stove for ten minutes. We sat and stared at the barnacle. The thing didn't budge. Not a millimeter. The salt wasn't doing anything to this one. It couldn't have cared less. I picked up an *In Shape* magazine off the coffee table and started paging through it.

"We've got a fighter," Phillip said.

The timer went off. Phillip walked over, brushed the salt away and tried to pull the barnacle off with his hands. All he ended up doing was lifting Jill off the couch by her butt.

"Fine," Jill said to me. "Get your damn crowbar."

I ran outside. The crowbar was sitting in the bed of the truck and it was pretty cold. On the way back into the house, I warmed the metal in my hands. Then I handed it to Phillip.

"Don't fuck up my skin," Jill warned. "Be delicate."

Phillip tried to slide the crowbar under the barnacle. Jill twisted around to watch Phillip work the handle, try to get some leverage.

It didn't look like anything was happening at first, but then a few seconds later Phillip got underneath the barnacle and it spun loose. There was this high pitched sucking sound right before it let go—like the last of the water going down a tub drain.

After it let go, there was an absolute mess of grey sludge left on Jill's butt. After Phillip wiped the goo away, there was a dark purple mark that looked like a hickey.

"I'm screwed," Jill said. "No way that's gone before tomorrow."

Phillip picked the barnacle off the floor and handed it to me. I felt the thing start trying to attach itself to my palm.

"Get rid of it," Phillip said.

I was going to throw the barnacle on the highway and let a car run over it and be done with all of this, but for some reason I couldn't. I looked at its knobby shell and for some reason throwing it on the road felt cruel and inhumane.

"I'll be back," I said.

I crossed the highway and made my way down the path to the beach. When I came to the water's edge, I stripped off my clothes. I ran into the ocean and swam out past the surf, to where the water got calm and glassy.

I wanted to say something to the barnacle then, something about how I was giving him a second chance and that he should use it wisely, but everything I thought of saying sounded stupid. In the end, I decided not to say anything. I just pulled him off my palm and dropped him into the ocean. I treaded water and watched him sink down into the murk.

I swam back. When I got close to the beach I saw Phillip waiting for me. My calf had cramped up and I sort of rolled out of the ocean and flopped down into the sand.

"You okay?" Phillip asked.

I nodded. Phillip had brought a blanket, and after I'd caught my breath, I stood up and he wrapped it around me and we walked back up to the house.

All that night, my brother put moisturizer on Jill's butt. Every moisturizer we had in the house—burn creams, facial masks, wrinkle removers—all night spreading stuff on that mark. Massaging it into Jill's skin. Hoping that ass hickey would disappear before the morning.

When I went to bed, the mark was so purple that I didn't think there was any chance that it would go away. Jill wasn't going to win the bikini contest with that.

I slept like the dead, tired from the swimming. When I woke up in the morning, I went out to the living room to check on the progress. Phillip was still rubbing.

"I've been up all night," he said. "Somehow she slept through most of it."

Phillip's huge hand was still covering up the spot, but then he lifted it up suddenly, like he'd performed a magic trick.

"Ta-da," he said.

The hickey had nearly disappeared. All that remained was a faint brown circle. It looked like a birthmark now, something that you could not help, something that over time might just fade away.

HOMECOMING

We were going to brunch, but my mother came down to the hotel lobby still dressed in her hotel robe. Her hair was all ratted out and she was limping, her left leg dragging behind her right.

"Jesus," I said. "You aren't ready yet?"

My mother was in Ann Arbor for homecoming. This was an annual thing. Every year her group of divorcees took a party bus from the Upper Peninsula on Friday night and then on Saturday, before the football game, they got hot stone massages and pedicures. After the game, they drank tequila and flashed their tits to any frat boy who yelled loud enough.

"There's a bit of a situation upstairs," she told me. "I need your help."

She grabbed onto my arm and leaned on me as we made our way to the elevator. The elevator was glass and as we rose I stared at her reflection. Our faces were nearly identical, my mother's and mine. Even though we looked so much alike, I had always done certain things with my hair and clothes to try and make sure no one realized this fact. This morning, my bangs were swept up into something that looked like a cresting wave and I had a black silk scarf tied very tightly around my neck.

"What's with that awful scarf?" my mother asked me. "And who told you those bangs worked?"

"No one told me anything," I said.

We got off the elevator and walked to her room. One of the lights in the hall was flickering and there was a high heel sitting in the middle of the floor. My mother slid her key card into the lock and swung open the door.

"Over there," she pointed.

The blinds were closed, but in the darkness I could see something huge lying on the bed. When I stepped closer, I saw that it was a naked man who had a gigantic exclamation point painted on his chest.

"I thought he would be out of here before now," my mother told me. "But this fucking whale just won't wake up."

I was in love with an architect named Gary. He was married and he had a beautiful seven-year-old daughter named Samantha. Recently, I'd met Samantha without Gary's permission. This was the reason I was wearing the silk scarf around my neck.

I had gone to Samantha's school a couple of times. There was a playground with a tube slide and some climbing ropes. After school, the kids who did not take the bus home waited there until their parents picked them up. Samantha was a pretty girl with a thin upturned nose and long skinny legs. She looked like her mother and not Gary, who was short and had a large nose and a barrel chest and who thought that when he yelled he was talking in a regular way. I liked to watch Samantha on the playground. She ran up and down the slides, flipped expertly along the monkey bars.

I usually drove over to Samantha's school and sat in my car and pretended like I was reading the newspaper, but I had recently purchased a very realistic looking fake baby off the Internet and had begun to put the baby in a stroller and sit on a bench near the playground. The baby was quite heavy and had eyelids that would stay closed if you wanted them to stay closed. If you picked up the baby, it flopped around like a real baby did.

The other day when I went there, I sat near where Samantha was playing on the swings. At one point, she walked over and stood staring at the fake baby.

"Babies sure sleep a lot," I said. "Way more than you might imagine."

There were other kids around, some of the school staff, other parents. I had dressed the fake baby in a pink onesie and put a sunhat on its head to cover up most of its face. Samantha came closer. She crouched down and tried to see the fake baby's face underneath the hat.

"Can I hold her if she wakes up?" she asked.

"Of course you can," I said.

Samantha kept on crouching lower and lower to try to get a better look at the baby's face.

"What's her name?" she asked me.

I had not named the fake baby yet. I had not even thought of naming it because in the end, what was the point of naming a fake baby? Still, a name came to me very quickly.

"Her name is Samantha," I said.

I sat down on the desk chair in my mother's hotel room. I readjusted my scarf. My mother rolled up a dirty pair of her pants and stuffed them into her suitcase. She took a brush and started to comb it through her gnarled hair.

"Just so you know, I'm not going to apologize," she said. "I have needs, just like you."

It felt like the scarf was slipping down on my neck and so I got up and went into the bathroom. I locked the door and I untied the scarf and looked at myself in the mirror. The bruises on my neck looked much more purple than they had earlier that morning.

"What are you doing in there?" my mother asked through the door. "Are you puking again?"

I climbed up on the toilet and looked out the tiny bathroom window. I thought about all of the movies and television shows where people climb out of bathroom windows to escape some uncomfortable or dangerous situation. Sometimes people got caught trying to climb out of them. Or sometimes they got stuck because their butts were just too big. Sometimes they made it, though. Sometimes the person in the hotel room broke down the bathroom door and the person they thought was going to be there had disappeared from their lives forever.

"I don't do that any more," I yelled back. "Remember? I'm cured of it."

I heard my mother's hoop earring scrape against the wood of the door. I retied the scarf tighter around my neck, tight enough so I could feel my pulse in my teeth.

"Where did he come from?" I asked her.

"There were a bunch of them at the game," my mother said. "They all had letters painted on their chests. When they stood in the right order they spelled out 'Go Wolverines,' with an exclamation point at the end. And this beautiful soul was the exclamation point."

Samantha's mother did not pick Samantha up from school that day she first talked to me. Gary drove up in his convertible. Gary had told me earlier in the week that he was going to Sacramento on a business trip, but here he was, *not* in Sacramento on a business trip. When Gary saw me on the playground, standing there with the stroller, he did not come over to me right away. First he called out to Samantha and got her safely into his car. Then he jogged back over to where I stood.

"Are you trying to fuck everything up?" he asked.

Gary was angry, but he had a grin on his face the entire time, so that anyone looking at us would think that we were old friends, chatting about tax cuts or baseball.

"I come here sometimes," I told him. "It's no big deal."

Gary knelt down and lifted the fake baby's sunhat off its head. He took his car key and poked it into the baby's skull. The baby's skull puckered inward, but when Gary pulled the key away the baby's head returned back to normal.

"What the hell is this?" he asked.

"I can stop," I told him. "I can stop coming here if that's what you want."

Gary was wearing leather driving gloves and he began to clench and unclench his hands. He looked back over at Samantha. Then he looked back at me. Then he jogged back over to his car and drove away.

When I came out of the bathroom, my mother wrapped her arms around me. It was supposed to be a hug, but I just stood there limp-armed while she squeezed. She brought her nose right near my mouth, sniffing my breath like she did when I was younger. All the enamel had come off my teeth and she had paid for veneers. She never let me forget it.

"What's this new one's name?" she asked. "The architect."

"Gary," I told her.

The blinds were drawn, but the wind pushed them away from the windowsill and the room lit up around us.

"He sounds made-up," she said. "From the stuff you told me, he sounds too good to be true."

I was suddenly worried that she was going to make me prove

that Gary existed. I didn't know if I could. There were no photos of us together. He never left me any voicemails. He'd never emailed or texted me. As far as anyone knew, Gary did not know that I existed. No one knew whether or not he loved or even liked me.

My mother limped over to the bed slowly, holding her hip with her hand.

"Dumbass here was on top of me for part of it," she said. "Big mistake."

She stood over the man with the exclamation point and then she smacked her hand on his belly. It echoed through the room, but the man did not stir. His penis was stuck to his thigh and he had these tiny nipples the size of dimes. It looked like if you rubbed them hard enough you might be able to rub them right off. My mother grabbed a disposable camera from the end table. She curled up on the bed next to the man. She threw her leg over his stomach and snapped a picture.

"All the ladies will want details," she explained. "And I don't want to disappoint."

Gary came by my apartment late last night. Instead of leaving the fake baby in the trunk like usual, I had carried it inside. It was lying facedown on my coffee table. Gary picked it up by the leg, shook it at me.

"I don't even know where to start with this," he said. "I really fucking don't."

Gary had redecorated my apartment for me. We'd gone to a furniture store one afternoon and he had picked out everything that I should buy. He was a modern architect, which meant that everything looked nice, but when you sat down on something it made your butt hurt.

"I just wanted Samantha to get to know me," I explained. "I wanted us to get acquainted before you and I are together for good."

After I said this, Gary walked over to me and ran his hand down my cheek. He did this very tenderly. He brought his other hand up to the back of my neck and began to massage my shoulders.

At first I thought all was forgiven, that we would be able to forget this incident and move on. I imagined that Gary and I would end up rolling around in my modern-looking bed very shortly. I decided that I would put on those garters that Gary had bought me and show him how much I loved him by doing that thing that he liked me to do but that I did not particularly like to do.

While I was thinking these things, Gary stopped massaging me. He brought his hands together around my throat and squeezed. He lifted me off the ground and pressed me into the wall. I tried to scream, but nothing would come out of my mouth.

"This is all your fault," he said before he dropped me down onto the carpet. "You couldn't just leave well enough alone, could you?"

My mother got into the shower. I sat down by the window and stared down at the street. There was a huge truck with a hose mounted on the front spraying down the sidewalk. I looked over at the exclamation point on the man's chest. From where I sat now, the exclamation point was upside down. It looked like some sort of ancient symbol, something painted on a cave wall that needed to be deciphered.

My mother came out of the bathroom dressed in jeans and a t-shirt. She had her hair slicked back. She picked up the disposable camera off the table, put on her jacket.

"There is a one-hour photo place across the street," she said. "I'm going to run over there quick."

"I'll go with you," I told her.

"Just stay here," she told me. "Stay here and make sure he doesn't steal anything."

I didn't want to stay, but I didn't really want to move either. I had tied the scarf too tightly. I was having trouble breathing. My body felt exhausted, my body felt like it was fading away. I felt like I was a capsule of cold medicine and someone had split me open and was dumping all my colorful innards onto the floor.

"Fine," I told my mother. "Hurry up."

When my mother left I untied my scarf. I walked over to the mirror by the dresser and looked at my neck. The bruises had turned from purple to dark black.

I was massaging the skin around my windpipe when I heard the man with the exclamation point cough. I turned toward him and he sat up. He looked around the room, his eyes watery and unable to focus. He arched his back, his stomach puffing out.

"Where is this?" he asked.

"This is Ann Arbor," I said.

He blinked his eyes, rubbed them with his palms. He scratched at one of his tiny nipples.

"I slept with my contacts in," he said. "I can't see for shit right now."

I did not want to look directly at him, but for some reason I did not want him to know that I would not look directly at him, so I focused on the painting that was just above his head. It was a landscape of a wheat field with a red brick house in the distance. It was harvest time in the painting. I tried to look inside the windows of the house, but there was nothing there, no lights or candles, just darkness.

"What's your name?" he asked.

The street-cleaning crew was across the street now. I was not going to tell him anything about me. I was not going to explain to him that it was my mother he'd fucked, not me. I was not going to explain to him that my mother was gone now, getting some photos developed that would prove this fact, that when she got back here he would see just how badly he was mistaken and that no words of apology would be enough to make me forgive him.

"Okay, that's cool," he said. "I get it. No names. We're on the lowdown."

The man slid over and sat on the edge of the bed. His stomach doubled over and part of the exclamation point disappeared into the folds. When he saw the bruises on my neck, his face pinched up and his eyes narrowed.

"Did I do that to you?" he asked.

There was a group of men pushing their brooms down the sidewalk, three men side by side, finishing off what the hose had already started. The streets below were clean. Like there had been no game, like no one had cheered and jumped up and down, like no one had drank and yelled until they'd lost their voices.

"Did I do that to you?" the man asked me again.

I retied the scarf around my neck and walked across the street to the one-hour photo place. I found my mother sitting in a chair by the counter. I sat down in a chair next to her.

"He's gone," I said.

"How did you get rid of him?" she asked.

"I don't know," I told her. "I just did."

As I sat there, I watched the photos slide out of the processing machine. The overhead lighting brought out all my mother's flaws—the forehead scar that looked like a frown, a black hair that was growing inside her ear.

I went into my purse. I'd stuck the fake baby's head in there and now took it out and handed it to her.

"What's this?" she asked.

"I found it on the way over," I told her.

She turned the baby's head over in her hand. She studied it

closely. She played with the baby's eyelids and ran her finger inside its ear.

"It's creepy looking," she said. "It looks so real."

I laid my head on my mother's shoulder. She ran her fingers through my hair as I sat there and watched the photos slide out of the developer and fall on top of each other, again and again, until they were in a big pile.

PROTOCOL

At the cusp of the first switchback are the leg traps. They're hidden under pine straw, jaws still set. Occasionally, you'll find something caught—a raccoon or a grouse—and carry it on up.

For the gauntlet of trip wires near the salt caves, you stretch onto your belly and scuttle through the red clay. Up the path, your breath gathers in front of you in tiny fists. You slip the cattle gate, move past the blue tarp that covers the woodpile. Protocol here is to push the doorbell mounted on the gatepost, but you keep your hands stuffed inside your parka and walk on. You hawk a loogie onto the septic tank and slink up the rickety porch stairs.

Through the steel door, you hear your father yell. Then there's the back and forth of a saw. When the sawing stops, there's more yelling. Then there's the saw again.

You light a menthol you stole from your Aunt Ginny's purse and you lift your hand and pound on the door. The saw and yelling stop. You hear boots scurrying over planks, a shotgun being ripped from its rack.

Instead of calling out to your father to stop what's next, you just stand there. You take another drag off your cigarette. You blow a mint-flavored breath and you close your eyes and wait for it.

Earlier that night, you and Frog and Harder were down by the river bluffs. Frog had stolen two cans of Reddi Whip from the restaurant where he worked and the three of you sucked through the cream to get to the nitrous. When the cans were cashed, you shotgunned the tiny bottles of liquor that Harder had kiped from his flight attendant mom. Each time one of you finished a bottle you dropped it off the cliff, listened to it plinko down through the limestone crags. There were shrooms too. Big hairy looking fuckers that felt like a piece of rubber on your tongue.

You watched as Frog heaved a huge slab of limestone into the river. It splashed down and you saw the water around the splash curl and ripple. You followed that patch of water as it got pulled downstream over the dam. This was the first time you'd hung out with Frog and Harder in the last few months. You suspect you will drift further apart once they decide on a college and you decide whatever it is that you are going to decide.

"So much water," you said.

You stood there and watched the river flow past you. You thought about jumping, getting a head of steam and hurling yourself out into the water. You thought about taking your wallet out of your pocket and chucking it into the middle of the river.

"Let's go fuck something up!" Harder yelled before you did either.

Harder had made varsity football in the fall and there was still a rash on his forehead from where his helmet dug into his skull. You watched him pull off a glove with his teeth, rake his fingernails over the rash. It had started out as a red splotch the size of a dime and it had grown throughout the season, annexing more and more skin.

Frog opened his trunk and pulled out a duffel bag. He unzipped it and tilted it toward you to reveal a cache of spray paint, dozens and dozens of different colored cans.

Frog looked like a frog in elementary school, with his bowl cut and his flared nostrils and those puffy lips, but not any longer. His hair was pulled back in a ponytail, his face had narrowed, girls now considered his lips kissable.

"Let's do this shit," he said.

For the next hour the three of you drove all over town transforming speed limit signs from a snail-paced thirty miles per hour into a fast and furious eighty. All it took was a couple arcs of spray paint.

The thing that set you off tonight was seemingly insignificant. While you were driving you saw a man riding a bike who looked exactly like your father. The same long grey wad of hair hanging around his shoulders, the same leathery skin. Since your mother died, you've been seeing things like this more often. You see men who resemble your dad, women who look like your mom. Usually it is only in small ways—the way their mouth folds when they smile or how they hold a cigarette up to their face or tap their foot nervously on the ground when they are sitting in a booth at a restaurant.

What happened tonight is that when you passed this man he turned and waved at you. It was a strong and hearty wave. Neighborly. The man held his hand up and shook it back and forth as you drove by. The man looked exactly like your dad, but this wave was something that your dad would never do.

"Did you see that?" you asked Frog and Harder.

"Did we see what?" Harder asked you.

And then, nothing.

Or at least not the nothing you expected. The nothing you expected involved a deafening bang and then a gaping hole in your head or gut. In that nothing, there would be vast amounts of blood gushing from the gaping hole and your dad would kneel over your body yelling shit, shit, shit, finally paying you some mind.

Or on second thought — maybe the nothing would be instantaneous. A sudden cut to static like when the TV at your aunt and uncle's house lost the cable feed.

Instead of either of these nothings, the cabin door flies open and your father stands in front of you, your shoot-first-ask-questions-later father not shooting first and not needing any questions later.

"How many times did we go over the approach protocol, Junior?" he says, lowering the sawed-off. "A million times? And then you forget to push the goddamn buzzer?"

Underneath your parka, you feel your ribcage heaving up and down like bellows stoking a fire. You wanted it, you still want it, but you realize now that there is something untappable inside you that will always cause you to fight it.

"I didn't forget anything," you tell him.

"The hell you didn't. I didn't hear any buzzer."

Your father wipes his eyes with his palm. His right eye is rimmed in goo, what you know right away is a wicked case of pink eye.

"I peeped you through the peephole," he says. "Otherwise, you'd be cooked."

You're wearing his old Army parka, the green one with the fur-lined collar and the name "Lowe" on the lapel. The parka was big before, but you haven't eaten much in the last three days and it swims around you, a noisy sea of green nylon and down.

"Lucky I looked," your father says.

He's wearing those half-gloves where the fingers are free. His beard has grown so unruly that you can't see his lips underneath the hair.

"Lucky you looked," you say.

– – – – – – – –

After Frog and Harder dropped you off, you went inside your aunt and uncle's house. You took the keys to your uncle's truck from the ceramic bowl on the kitchen counter. You told yourself that you were just going to go for a drive to clear your head. But when you started to drive you thought about the waving man and you kept on driving until you turned off the county road and headed north. You took the turnoff to Miller's Peak and put the truck in towing gear. You found yourself bumping down the loamy ruts that led to the clearing below your father's cabin. You shoved the truck into park and you tied your shoes and started up the trail.

Inside the cabin, the potbelly stove belches out a thin trail of smoke. There's a window near the kitchen table where you sit that looks out on the back of your father's lot. From there, you get the lay of the land. The junipers weighed down by shingles of November snow, the tank of brownish bio-diesel, the chicken coop. When the wind dies down, you hear the hum of the generator.

"Isn't this a school night?" he asks.

You keep your parka zipped up and your gloves and stocking cap on. Your feet are frozen and you stomp them on the floor to get the blood moving.

"No school tomorrow," you lie. "Teacher conferences."

Your father grabs a dishtowel and buries his eyes inside it.

"I've been waiting to become a martyr," he tells you. He yanks the dishtowel away from his face now, like he's playing peek-a-boo. "I think it's my big day and then I look through the peephole and it's my own damn kid."

He gets up from the table and chucks a piece of wood into the stove. He stokes the fire with the poker, slams the hatch. Truthfully, inside the cabin's not much better than out. Even though there's been an attempt inside here to divert the Northerlies—the cracks in between the walls stuffed full of newspaper, porn, empty potato chip bags, and old pairs of your father's crusty y-fronts—there's still a high-pitched whistle between the clapboards.

"You need an eye-opener?" he asks. He lifts a bottle of moonshine and holds it up to you. He shakes the bottle, tick-tock, swishes around the piss-colored liquid inside. You nod. Your father pulls two Mason jars off the shelf and carries them to the table. He pushes shotgun shells and copper wire aside and he rolls up a piece of butcher paper with a large penciled drawing of what looks to be a prototype for a land mine.

"I'm probably contagious," he tells you. "Just walking in here you probably got what I got."

Your eyes scan the room. The shelf of canned goods, the boxes of powdered milk, the summer pickles swimming in their brine. Underneath all the foodstuffs are neatly stacked boxes of ammo. On the bottom shelf are the pamphlets that your dad distributes to his mailing list.

Most of them you've committed to memory—"Free the Presses! SCREW the Taxman!" "What Your Tax Dollars REALLY Support!" and "Going Off The Grid: WHAT YOU NEED TO KNOW!" They are written with such urgency, exclamation points and capital letters everywhere. To properly read one of them out loud, you'd have to yell.

You see the torn up mattress then. The white fluff busting from its insides, the wayward springs, the piles of down littered across the floorboards. Things like this don't surprise you anymore—your father guts furniture all the time. Most times you come up here he gives you the pat-down hug, the kind you get when someone thinks you are wired for sound.

"What's with the bed?" you ask.

"The bed's been compromised," he says.

You sip the moonshine. Your dad moves to the sink. He grabs a Brillo pad and scrubs off the griddle. The bottle is in front of you and you tip it and fill your Mason jar again. You watch your father's brown cords slide down his ass until you can see the crack. They haven't been washed in weeks, these pants, they have a greasy sheen on them like bear fur. Your father yanks his pants up again and again as he scrubs, but they never stay where they should.

You think about leaving again, hiding out in the woods for an hour or two and then coming back and knocking on the door unannounced one more time. Maybe this time you'd yell "ATF!" in a deep voice. Maybe that would work.

You slide your belt off and hold the piece of leather out to your old man. It takes a second for your father to figure out that you are giving him the belt to keep and when he does he shakes his head no.

"I am sick of seeing your asscrack," you tell him. You sit back down and take a pull of moonshine straight from the bottle. Your father stands there holding the belt in his hand like it's a snake that's just had the life wrung out of it.

After a while, like you'd hoped, the room starts to spin and then begins to dip and roll. You set your head down on the table, shut your eyes.

You wake up to the back and forth of the saw. You see your father kneeling over the mattress, shirtless now, clumps of down stuck to his sweaty chest. It's like the man's molting, morphing into something new.

There's a big puddle of drool next to you on the table. You rub your eyes, pinch the crust from the corners.

Your father nods and then he turns away from you and resumes his sawing, *ZZeeeZZaaa, ZZeeeZZaaa*, back and forth.

You stumble over to the sink, cup your hands under the faucet, splash water on your face. You look out on the overcast sky, the clouds blocking the morning light. There's a hunting knife in the drying rack and you grab onto the handle. A chill spreads up your chest and you have to steady yourself on the kitchen counter.

"You gonna puke?" your father asks. You look at him. His eyes are teary, surrounded by that all pink puss.

"No," you tell him even though you can feel the salt rising up from your stomach into the back of your throat. "No way."

You grip the knife and stumble over to the bed. Your father stops sawing and watches you.

"Are you okay?" he asks.

You ignore him. You wrap your fingers around the handle of the knife and then you lift it up into the air and ram it down into the mattress. You twist the blade out and then you slam it down again.

"What are you waiting for?" you ask your father. He nods and then he picks up his saw and the two of you claw and rip and pull and gouge that mattress like there is someone trapped inside it, someone trapped inside that desperately needs to breathe.

SHOO, SHOO

Shoo, shoo, my wife said, but those were not the words. Quite obviously those were not the words. We might as well have thrown a bottle of Jack and a dime bag of skunk weed down from our bedroom window and said, Hunker down fellas, stay awhile. These were jazz musicians and my wife had said shoo.

Earlier that day, we'd gotten the test results. It ended up being both of our faults. Her eggs were bad and my sperm was lazy. We sat in the parking lot of the clinic for about an hour after our appointment, in that car of ours that you started with a screwdriver and stopped by pulling up on the emergency brake. I paged though a glossy pamphlet that made adoption look cool and fun.

"I was ready to blame you and then *pretend* I wasn't blaming you," she said. "I was ready to blame myself and then not believe you when you said it wasn't my fault."

"Exactly," I told her.

"I really don't know what to do now," she told me.

"Totally," I said.

- - - - - - - -

I'd already called the cops. I'd already held the phone out the window and let the police dispatcher listen to the racket below, the joshing and stumbling and bellowing and knee slapping and the occasional horn bleat and rim shot.

"In my neighborhood, noise like that would be welcome," the dispatcher told me. "I'd love to hear some noise like that sometime."

I hung up the phone and kneaded my wife's shoulders, pushing against the braids of her back muscle until I found bone.

"Maybe we could have a miracle baby," I offered. "One of those against-all-odds babies that never should have happened. Everyone else has them," I said, "why not us?"

After I said this, my wife got up and put on her robe. I watched as she began to drag our dresser across the bedroom floor. It was huge, this dresser, claw-footed, an heirloom, passed down from her grandmother and her grandmother's grandmother before that.

"What are you doing?" I asked.

I watched as she lifted the dresser on the windowsill and then pushed it out the window. There was a loud crash, then a clattering of instruments, then voices yelling out below. My wife walked across the room and lifted up a bedside table and then tossed that out as well.

The musicians had run off by then, gone to wherever it is jazz musicians go when people get tired of their shenanigans, but my wife kept on—the good silverware, the coffee pot, those super sharp knives I bought off TV.

I got up and went into the bathroom. I took wet toilet paper and stuffed it into my ears. I laid down on the linoleum floor. I closed my eyes and listened to my heart echo all around me.

THE EGG

Scott lived on the point of a lake. The lake was part of a chain of lakes that from above looked like fingers on a hand. Scott and his father usually swam in the lake, except when there was heron shit on the beach and they were forced to swim in their indoor pool. If you screamed in the pool it echoed off the walls, but if you screamed on the banks of the lake the pine trees swallowed up the sound. Scott's father often told Scott that lake swimming was one of the simple joys that everyone, no matter what their station in life, could enjoy.

One thing his father enjoyed more than swimming in the lake was firing people. Two summers ago, Scott canoed across the lake and burned down a cemetery and his father had fired Scott's nanny. Another time Scott's boa constrictor, Rusty Jones, died choking on their neighbor's pet rabbit and his father fired Scott's other nanny. Last summer, Scott's older brother, Donald, had climbed up on the roof above the pool to break into the house to steal money for needle drugs and he had fallen through the roof and drowned. The morning after, Scott's father fired everyone: the pool man, his security firm, his handyman and Scott's new nanny, Pilar, who'd only been taking care of Scott for two days.

Sometimes Scott's father went swimming in the lake even when there was heron shit all over the beach. When his father did this, he came inside and itched himself raw. Sometimes his father soaked in the hot tub to stop the itching and moaned Donald's name loud enough to wake Scott from sleep. When this happened Scott wished that his father would just go down to the beach and moan there, where no one would hear or care.

As far as Scott was concerned, he was having a good childhood. His mother had died from a brain tumor shortly after he was born, but since he did not know her, it did not make him particularly sad. He knew that his mother was pretty and he knew that he resembled her in the way his eyelids sank over his dark eyes and in the way his upper lip curled. He looked like Donald in the way his chin clefted and his curly brown hair cowlicked over his forehead.

Scott was sadder about Donald's death than about his mother's death, but he was not horribly sad about either of them. Scott was much younger than Donald and most of the time Scott had spent with Donald recently involved Donald nodding off in the middle of a story or tearing apart Scott's room looking for Scott's secret money sock.

What Donald and Scott usually spoke about before Donald had died was their dad. Donald blamed him for everything in his life that had gone wrong. He would sit in Scott's computer chair and drool onto Scott's computer keyboard and tell Scott about how their father was going to ruin his childhood.

"Really?" Scott asked.

"It's inevitable," Donald told him. "He's cursed and he makes sure that you share in his bad luck."

"He seems fine to me," Scott said. "Better than fine."

"He's an absentee parent," Donald said. "He hides his love away like it is some sort of treasure."

Scott did not agree with his brother that his dad was ruining his childhood. Scott's life that summer consisted of eating anything he wanted and playing video games for hours on end. He could paddle his canoe out to the small islands in the finger lakes and spear birds or fish with the spear he'd found in the garage. He could also shoot birds or fish with the pellet gun he'd gotten last year for his birthday. Just as long as he did not burn anything else down and just as long as he buried anything endangered that he shot or speared, he would not be in any trouble with his dad.

The only thing Scott was absolutely forbidden to do was go into his father's office when his father was away on business. But whenever Scott's new nanny, Rosarita, fell asleep on the couch in front of the television, Scott snuck downstairs and picked the office lock with a butter knife. Then Scott sat in his father's high-backed leather desk chair and sipped Dr. Pepper from a bendy straw.

One afternoon, while he was in the office, Scott picked up his father's ivory pen. The pen was cold and heavy and it felt similar to the spear he'd recently found in the back of the garage. Scott held up the pen under a desk lamp to get a closer look at it, but the pen was slippery and fell from his hand. The pen rolled under the desk and when he went to retrieve it, Scott found a red button sticking out of the floor.

Scott pressed down on the button with his hand and he heard the phone on his father's desk ring. He waited for the phone to ring again, but it did not. Scott pressed it again and the phone rang again. Scott got up from under the desk and picked up the receiver. There was no one on the other end of the line.

Scott sat back down in the chair like his father always did. He took a sip of his Dr. Pepper and reached his foot down to press the button. The phone rang and he picked it up. Scott said "This is Ron Jacobs" in a deep voice. Again, there was no one on the other end of the line—no dial tone, no busy signal, no one wanting to talk to his dad.

The phone looked like a real phone, with a phone's weight and heft, but when Scott followed the cord out the back of it he saw that it went down into a notch in the floorboards. And when he pulled on the cord it came out of the hole frayed, attached to nothing.

Scott's father traded currency. Sometimes at dinner his father would sit down at the dining room table and take out a piece of paper and a pen and draw some diagrams and try to explain to Scott what he did. Scott would yawn or wonder if he could go outside and play. Sometimes his father would get a call on his cell phone and then his food would sit there at the table until Rosarita carried his father's plate back to the kitchen.

Usually Rosarita ate dinner in the kitchen, but when his father took a phone call during dinner, Rosarita would bring her plate of food and sit down next to Scott.

"Will you take the canoe out tomorrow?" she asked him.

"I think I will," he told her.

Sometimes Scott woke up at night screaming. He usually did not remember the nightmares that made him yell out, but whenever he woke from them Rosarita would be there. She would stroke his hair until he fell back asleep. Sometimes his father would be there too, pacing back and forth outside his room, but he would never come into Scott's room.

"How come you don't come in my room after I've had a nightmare?" he asked his dad one night at dinner.

"Are you having nightmares?" his dad asked. "That's horrible."

"I see you outside my door," Scott said.

"You see me?" his dad said.

- - - - - - - -

Most days, when Scott got tired of being inside, he would go down to the lake and get into his canoe and paddle out to Gray's Island. He was not supposed to go to Gray's Island because it was a protected wetland and a nesting area for the endangered herons, but he dressed in a camouflage shirt and khaki shorts and wore a dark hat and sunglasses. When he got to the island he hid his canoe in the reeds. He had gotten close to one of the nests the last time he'd been there, but a mother heron had run at him, flapping her wings and squawking loudly. That time, Scott had not thrown his spear accurately. It had flown past the skinny bird and into the water of the channel. This time he tucked his pellet gun into the waistband of his shorts and if the bird charged him, he planned to take his time and shoot the bird right in its stupid face.

Scott slid his canoe onto the island and then he army crawled to the nest. The mother heron was not there. He got closer and saw that inside the nest were five speckled eggs, lying in a tightly packed half-circle. He lifted one up and shook it back and forth. It made a sloshing sound. He tapped on the shell with his finger and listened to the echo inside.

He knew the mother heron was going to return shortly, so he wrapped the egg in his shirt and stuffed it into his backpack. He ran back to the canoe and pushed off into the water. As he paddled away he stared up at the sky, waiting for the mother heron to swoop down and fight him for its baby, but the mother heron never came.

When he got home Scott grabbed a bath towel and wrapped it around the egg. He set the egg into Rusty Jones's old aquarium and turned on the snake's heat lamp to keep the egg warm.

"What did you do now?" Rosarita asked him when she came into his room. "Where did you get that?"

"I'm going to save it," he told her. "I am going to hatch it and raise it as my own."

Rosarita lifted up a picture and dusted off the top of Scott's desk. She had been in a bad car accident when she was younger. Scott often made her take off her shoe and show him where a steel rod ran down her leg. When she first told him, he did not believe that there was metal inside her body, so she stuck a magnet to her shin.

"I will always tell you the truth," she told him.

Scott went over and lifted the egg out of the aquarium. He held it out to her to hold, but she waved him off.

"You need to put the egg back where you found it," she told him. "Before there is legal trouble."

"It's mine now," he said. "It's not anyone else's anymore."

"Maybe I'll tell your father," Rosarita said. "Then we'll see?"

Scott knew that Rosarita would not tell his father. He'd recently peed off his bedroom balcony onto the top of an electrician's truck. Rosarita had threatened to tell his father about that, but hadn't followed through on her threat. Last week, she'd caught him in his father's office, pressing the red button on the floor and making the phone ring again and again. She hadn't said anything about that either.

"Go ahead and tell him," Scott told her.

Scott's father was traveling to Ecuador that morning to trade some currency. Before he left Scott went down to his office.

"I want a dog," he said.

Scott did not want a dog. And he knew that his father would not get him a dog because his father had just lost his two dogs, Chief and General, after they drank some anti-freeze that a mechanic had spilled in the garage.

"I want a Jack Russell," Scott said. "A white one with black and brown spots."

Scott's father nodded his head up and down and then Scott saw a slight movement in his father's thigh. The fake phone broke the silence.

"Hold that thought," his father said.

His father picked up the receiver and then spun his chair around away from Scott. His father's hair had turned white long ago, but he dyed it jet-black now.

"Señor Gonsalves," his father said. "¿Cómo está?"

Scott sat at the kitchen table and watched while Rosarita peeled carrots for dinner.

"It will be just you and me for dinner," she told him. "We can eat in front of the television if you want."

Rosarita once cut herself while chopping up a red pepper and when Scott begged her, she let him suck the blood from her thumb. He remembered how her blood tasted different than his, sort of salty, whereas his tasted sort of like dirt.

"If I cut myself would you suck some of my blood?" he asked Rosarita. "So we're even?"

Rosarita did not look up from the carrots. She peeled with long strokes and the orange skin curled into the garbage can. When she finished one of them, she set it in the colander in the sink.

"That was a mistake," she told him. "We don't do that ever again."

While she rinsed off the carrots, Scott walked over near her. He slid a knife out of the butcher block and pressed it into the tip of his index finger, splitting the skin. The blood came quickly to the cut and Scott snuck up behind Rosarita and pressed his finger onto Rosarita's lips.

Rosarita spun her head away from him and then spat into the sink. She took a washcloth and wiped her mouth with it.

"Why do you do these things?" she yelled.

- - - - - - - -

Scott checked on the egg every morning before breakfast and then at night before he went to sleep. He learned there was not much to do with an egg other than keep it warm. Occasionally when he was bored he would take it out and set it on the carpet of his bedroom and roll it across the floor with his foot. One day he took a pencil and wrote the word "Buddy" on the eggshell. This would be what he would name the bird. Either that or Merlin.

That night, even though there was bird shit all over the beach, Scott put on his trunks and went swimming. He jumped off the end of the dock and into the deep water. He dove down and rooted his hand around in the sandy bottom. A few months ago, he found a gold coin in the silt and when his father had a dinner party he had asked Scott to show it to some of the party guests.

Scott enjoyed holding the coin out to the guests and having these people look at it with excitement. Some of them asked him questions about the coin. Some of them laughed at how he answered their questions. His father was having another party next week and Scott wanted to find something else that was valuable and interesting enough to show to people. He dove and dove, but the only thing that he found was an old ceramic bowl. Rosarita called him for dinner, but he pretended not to hear her. He kept on diving and taking his hand and running it through the bottom of the lake.

He knew that if he waited long enough, Rosarita would bring his dinner down to the dock. Then he could sit with his feet in the water and eat his sandwich. His father often spoke of the appetite that comes after swimming, how food tasted different after you'd been in the water for a long time. Scott agreed that this was absolutely true.

Scott went to bed and then woke up later that night itching. He screamed and scratched and yelled for Rosarita.

"You and your father go into the lake when the *caca* is there," she said. "And you expect something different?"

She ran a bath for him and poured salts into the water. She sat on the toilet and waited for the itching to stop. When it did, she helped him out of the tub and wrapped a towel around his body.

Scott knew that Rosarita sent money home to her children each month. Once, she had shown him a picture of her husband and their children standing in front of a train station. Scott had held the picture for a long time, staring at their faces. He had not asked her what he wanted to ask her.

"Do you think they miss you?" he asked her now as he climbed into bed.

"Does who miss me?" she said.

"Your children," he said.

Rosarita pulled the blankets up to his chin and took her fingers and pushed his hair away from his eyes.

"It will not be like this forever," she said.

"It might be like this forever," Scott said. "You never know."

Rosarita let her hair down and then she gathered it back up into a ponytail. She got up from the bed and walked across the room and turned off the light.

"Can I sleep with the egg?" Scott asked her.

"You cannot sleep with the egg," she told him.

When his father came home from Ecuador, Scott asked him for a dog again. This time he found a picture on the Internet and showed it to his father. Scott made a good case for the dog. He told his father that a dog would teach him responsibility. He told him that he would take very good care of it, that he would feed it and that he would take it for walks. Scott said that if there were any vermin in the house the dog would certainly catch them or chase them into the water where they would drown or be eaten.

"This is what Jack Russells are bred for," he said. "Killing stuff."
He heard his father slide his foot across the floor. The phone rang.
"Ron Jacobs," his father said into the mouthpiece. "Talk to me."
His father covered the phone in his hand and then turned to Scott.

"Sorry, champ," he said. "But I've got to take this."

That night Scott's father left for another business trip. Scott broke into his office and sat in his desk chair. There were some herons hooting outside. No matter how many people his father hired and fired birds would always come back and shit on their beach.

Scott had taken some wood matches from the kitchen and he lit one and threw it into the wastebasket next to the desk. The paper inside the can started on fire. While it burned, Scott went upstairs and grabbed the egg from the aquarium. He brought it down and he set it on top of the desk and rolled it back and forth. He shook it, heard it slosh. The smoke from the garbage can was billowing up toward the ceiling. Scott lifted the egg up above his head and dropped it onto the desk. The egg split apart and a grey sludge spilled out of the shell and ran over the desk and onto the carpet. Scott ran his fingers through the slurry, trying to find something he could recognize, a feather or a beak. It was just goo inside, worse than water.

"Where are you?" he yelled.

Scott leaned back into his father's chair and he took his foot and pressed the red button on the floor. The fake phone rang. The smoke alarm went off, a horrible screech, but he plugged his ears. He kept pushing the red button. He wished Rosarita would hurry up and find him. He wished that she would put out the fire and then wrap her arms around him and carry him upstairs to bed.

WHISKERS

After Chloe's last suicide attempt, the one with the grapefruit knife, her father, Greer Burton, cleaned out the storage space above his garage. He horsed an exam table destined for scrap off the University Hospital's loading dock and bumped it up his back stairs with the hospital's dolly. He purchased a cut-rate X-ray machine from a shady Russian named Yuri over in Las Cruces and then conned Alice Trincado from Invidrogen into letting him demo the rest of what he needed. Two of the four chairs from his dining room were taken hostage and placed next to a coffee table he'd found at Goodwill. The magazines that he fanned out there were mostly old and mostly his dead wife's.

Small animals and exotics were examined upstairs. Anything large or bleeding Greer motioned into the vacant stall next to his Buick LeSabre.

One afternoon, as he hosed matted horse fur from the floor of his garage, three Mexicans drove up with a longhorn steer bumping around in the payload of their pickup.

"You that vet?" the driver of the truck yelled over the idling engine.

Greer looked over at Chloe. When she was upstairs, he handcuffed her to the radiator. When she was down here, he shackled her to the door handle of his car. He knew how bad it looked, but things were exactly this bad or worse. Something had unraveled in his daughter, and keeping her close was the only way he thought that everything in her might be spooled up again.

"You the vet?" the man asked him again.

"Sure," he said. "For now."

For the first month it was all word of mouth, this impromptu animal husbandry of Greer's. He'd taken a leave of absence from his immunology research at the University to take over Chloe's corporeal care. When money ran short, he'd let slip to a select few that he could take a look at their pets to make ends meet. He hadn't expected much more than the occasional dog or cat, but then people began to show up on his doorstep at all hours.

A Flemish rabbit with ears the length of Greer's entire arm. A yellow lab that had swallowed a ziplocked bag of weed. A man holding an entire pickle bucket full of angry white rats.

Whatever they brought, Greer did what he could. When he could not do anything he took some horse tranquilizer from his lockbox and made the animals very comfortable.

"You are just like a regular vet," everyone told him. "Except that you are way cheaper."

One Sunday in June, Greer's neighbor, Randy Wright, rolled up Greer's driveway. Greer watched from the dormer window as Randy pulled an antique birdcage out of the passenger seat of his Jeep and lugged a large blue bird up the stairs.

"I bought him from a street vendor two weeks ago," Randy said. "Thought the damn thing would be better company than a radio."

Chloe was sitting on the floor across the room. Her handcuffs clinked over the tines of the radiator whenever she shifted her body. The meds that Greer forced past her tongue each morning were giving her nosebleeds, and the two wads of Kleenex she had shoved up her nostrils protruded like small tusks. She wore one of Greer's old cowboy shirts with pearl snap buttons and a pair of his chinos that had faded to the color of twine. In the last few weeks most of her clothes had become spattered with blood—what her psychiatrist, Dr. Gupta, called "an unfortunate side effect of the side effects"—and now Greer had begun to raid his own closet, dress her in clothes he himself hadn't seen fit to wear in years.

"Gretchen says *hola*," Randy told Chloe.

Gretchen was Randy's daughter. She was the same age as Chloe, a rail-thin girl who before Wright's divorce Greer had often seen driving on the dirt road into town, her hands set rigidly on the wheel at ten and two. Gretchen had played on the same volleyball team as Chloe before Chloe started to stab and cut and swallow anything she could to help her depart the earth.

"Then tell her *hola* back," Chloe snapped.

Randy flopped down on the couch in the waiting area, pinched a mint from the candy dish.

"I'd apologize for Chloe's manners," Greer told him. "But it would just make it worse for both of us."

Wright nodded. The men had been semi-decent friends when Greer's wife, Cathy, was still alive. They had once gone on a golf junket in Myrtle Beach and gotten wasted enough one night to run naked into the ocean together. Since Cathy died and Randall split with Lisa, neither of them made much of an effort to remain friends.

Greer took a tongue depressor from the drawer in the exam table, pried open the bird's mouth.

"How long has he been like this?" Greer asked.

"Couple of days I guess," Randy said. "He's usually a funny son of a bitch. He knows a bunch of jokes. Before all this, I used to sit on the porch with a beer and have him tell me joke after joke. Damn thing really cheered me up."

Since Greer had opened this clinic, he had a sense that he'd missed his calling, that he had wasted his time in the lab with all of the bubbling Erlandmeyers and multi-channel pipettes and grant applications. He was much better with live animals. Science was exciting when he was younger, but now there was too much that was unknowable for him, things were too theoretical, there was too much idle chatter about whys and wherefores. His last few years in the lab felt like he was fumbling in the darkness for a light switch and that even when the light got turned on it was disappointing and sad, too dim to even make the roaches scatter.

Greer took a package of saltines from a cabinet drawer and set a couple in front of the parrot. The bird ambled toward the cracker. He poked his beak into a chunk of the cracker and leaned his head back and swallowed. After he finished the cracker, he opened his beak and whispered something. Greer leaned in, but what the bird said was too low and breathy for him to hear.

"What is he yakking about?" he asked Randy.

"Hell if I know," Randy told him. "I can't figure out anything he's been saying lately."

Greer got up and walked over to the corner of the room. Before he'd turned the garage into a clinic, before Chloe had begun to attempt suicide so often and in so many various and creative ways, her band, The Whorphans, had used it as a rehearsal space. All of their equipment remained—Cassidy's drums stacked under a tarp in the corner, Erica's keyboard tipped on its end along the south wall. After a month of concerned phone calls from the girls, they'd both stopped calling to check on Chloe's progress.

Greer plugged the microphone into the amp and held it up to the bird's mouth. The animal was a goner, he knew that for certain, but there was something else, a look in the bird's eyes that said he wanted to relay something very important to them before he passed on.

"What?" Greer asked the bird. "What's so goddamn urgent?"

Greer noticed that Chloe was staring at the bird, waiting to see what he would say. The shirt of his that she was wearing slipped down off her shoulder. She removed the Kleenex from her nose and she stuck out her lip so that the small stream of blood trickled right into her mouth.

Greer stood and watched the bird. The parrot opened his beak, but instead of anything cogent what came out was a bunch of unintelligible hisses and crackles. It sounded like words, but words that were missing all their vowels.

"I am going to find that street vendor and kick his ass," Randy said. "That's my next move here."

Greer stared down onto his driveway. He watched another car drive up and a man pull a small bear on a leash out of his back seat. Greer was already a little drunk and assumed that his eyes were playing tricks on him, that it was probably, in the end, just a fat brown dog.

He passed Randy the bottle of Jim Beam that he always sipped on while he worked in the garage. Randy took a long pull, wiped his mouth with his sleeve.

"Love him while he's alive to love," Greer told him.

Greer had hired a Dutch woman named Inge Hammaart to watch Chloe on Thursdays, while Greer played in a dart league with his former co-workers from the university. Inge came highly recommended from a colleague, Doug Wentz, who'd hired her for his wife, Beverly, who could not stop drinking rubbing alcohol. When they met the first time, Inge handed Greer a business card that read, "Inge Hammaart, Sober Companion." According to Chloe it might as well have also said "Shadowing Bitch."

"She makes me shit with the door open," she told Greer. "I have to push and grunt right in front of her fucking butter face."

Tonight on the way home from darts, Greer stopped off at

the convenience store and bought ice cream sandwiches. When he got home, Chloe was curled up on the couch under a blanket. Greer sat down next to her and slid his fingers into her short hair, something she had, up until a couple of months ago, loved, but now, like everything else, either ignored or railed against.

"How was she tonight?" he asked Inge.

"The same," Inge told him. "I try to play cards with her, but she never picks up her hand."

Inge went into the kitchen to gather up her purse and her coat. Chloe pushed Greer's hand out of her hair. She sat up and took a swallow of water. There was no calming his daughter now; she fought both affection and anger.

"I hate that fat dyke," she said. "Why would I play cards with someone who stares at my snatch when I take a piss?"

Greer unwrapped Chloe's ice cream sandwich for her. He sat down in the recliner next to the couch and while he ate his, he watched her chew and swallow. She'd gained weight in the last few weeks, had grown a little potbelly that paunched over his ancient pair of sweatpants, the ones that he'd worn all throughout grad school. Her belly was a positive thing, wasn't it?

"Maybe she's turning it around," he'd suggested to Dr. Gupta on their last visit. "She's eating better."

"More than likely she's trying to lull you to sleep before another opportunity presents itself," Dr. Gupta told him. "That's what she's all about right now. That's what she'll be about for a long time."

After Chloe finished eating, she got up and walked into the kitchen. Greer rose from his chair and followed right behind her. They were basically tethered to each other now. When her personal space had disappeared, his had too.

"She's the opposite of MacGyver," Inge had told him the other night. "Instead of saving herself by making a knife out of a bed spring, she'll use it to stab herself in the heart."

In a CD player by his bedside, Greer had the only recorded music that The Whorphans had ever made, a tinny sounding CD of three songs that were recorded at Scooter's—a teen club in town.

Most nights, after he crawled under his sheets, after he'd strapped Chloe into her bed with the leather straps he'd bought from a man in Ohio in an online auction, he popped the disc into the CD player.

"Maybe you could pick up your guitar later," he said to her now. "Maybe your guitar would help."

Another Saturday, a couple of weeks after the parrot, a man named Karpus showed up wanting to connect a pair of hawk's wings to his cat. The hawk was dead, his cat was not. Karpus cradled the cat in the crook of his elbow. It would meow for a bit, but then it would cough. Greer thought the coughing sounded bizarre. It sounded nearly human, like an old codger with late stage emphysema.

"Are you kidding?" Greer asked. "Is this some sort of joke?"

Karpus took the dead hawk out of his briefcase and set it gently down on the exam table.

"This bird's been dead about fifteen minutes," Karpus said. Greer looked at the hawk. It had a tread mark running down its abdomen, but the wings were still intact.

"If Whiskers could talk he would tell you that this was his dying wish," Karpus explained. "To be able to finally fly."

This line even got a chuckle out of Chloe. She was paging through a magazine and Greer turned around to look at her just in time to see her roll her eyes.

Undeterred, Karpus spread out fifty crisp one hundred dollar bills on the operating table. Greer tried not to look at the money, but then Karpus picked it up and waved it in front of Greer's face. Whenever Greer saw money lately he immediately thought about how much Inge cost, how his mortgage was killing him, how much Chloe's meds ran every month, even with the co-pay.

"You understand that this is never going to work," he told Karpus. "You know that, right?"

Greer knocked the cat out, made a small incision above his shoulder blade. He'd thought this procedure over for a total of about ten seconds. He knew this was not going to work—the cat would die within the week, either from trauma or infection—but he'd been sneaking pulls from his bottle of Beam all afternoon and he was just drunk enough not to care.

Karpus sat down across the room. He looked over at Chloe sitting there with her wrist handcuffed to the radiator. She had dozed off, her mouth wide open, a bead of drool in the corner of her mouth that extended all the way to the floor.

"What's with the girl?" Karpus asked him. "You a kidnapper too?"

Greer ignored him. He took a scalpel and sliced the wings off the hawk. He trimmed the wings back until he thought he had viable tissue. He began to suture the first wing onto the cat, weaving a needle in and out of the opening in its back.

Whiskers looked dead, his tongue flopping out the side of his mouth, his hips splayed wide open. His breath was soldiering on, though, his little cat stomach moving up and down nice and regular. After he'd attached the second wing, Greer closed up the cat, wrapped and taped the wings to his torso.

"If he's breathing in two weeks," Greer said, "then bring him back."

During the next week or so, Chloe seemed to improve. Greer didn't know if it was her new round of meds starting to find their way into the dark recesses of her brain or if she was honest-to-God feeling better about life and its prospects, but a couple of nights after he'd operated on Whiskers, Chloe went over and picked up her electric guitar, tuned it and then strummed out a few chords.

"Are you taking requests?" Greer asked her.

"It depends on what you request," she said.

"How about 'Crush All the Venture Capitalists'?" This was Greer's favorite Whorphans song. It had a driving guitar and pounding drums and Chloe's piercing voice screaming over the top of it all.

She brought her guitar up and strummed a few chords slowly, searching her brain for the rhythm. She paused for a second, but then suddenly she jumped right into it. She thrashed out the chords and then screamed out the first verse. When she was just about to get to the chorus, Greer's favorite part, her voice trailed off.

"That's all I can remember right now," she said.

The color that she'd had in her cheeks a moment ago had drained away. Greer saw a trickle of blood snake out of her nostril. He handed her a paper towel and she wiped it away.

"Maybe you can try again later," he said.

She slumped down on the couch and closed her eyes. She wrapped her arms around her body and sat there holding herself, like there was a leak inside her body that she was trying to stop.

"Maybe," she said.

Karpus showed up two weeks later with Whiskers. He was still alive, but barely. Greer had wrapped Whiskers' wings tight to his body and when he cut away the tape the cat's new wings flopped out and hit the floor. The stitches looked like they had actually taken root. For a minute or two they all stood there and watched Whiskers walk around. It was clear that the cat couldn't figure out what was going on. His wings were dragging on the floor and the cat spun in a tiny circle trying to get a better look at them.

Greer was tired and he wanted to get rid of the cat, get rid of Karpus, but then Greer saw the wings move. It was just a quick movement, almost a twitch, the cat lifting them up off the floor a millimeter or two, but once Whiskers did it, once the wings lifted, his cat lips pursed into what Greer could have sworn was a grin. Karpus saw this too.

"I told you!" he yelled.

Chloe had been watching all this. She stood up and pulled at her handcuffs to get a closer look. Greer went over and unlocked her and she stood next to Greer and they watched the cat move around the room, each time lifting his wings a little higher.

"I want to go out to your roof," Karpus said. "I want to go now."

Greer wanted to argue, he wanted to tell Karpus to wait until the cat got stronger or to find some other place, a high cliff or a tall building, but he knew Karpus wouldn't listen to him. He realized that they were too far down this road to do anything other than take the cat up to the third floor of his house and toss him off and see what happened.

"I suppose you want to go up there too?" he asked Chloe.

Greer knew that she was going to try to jump, that those wheels were moving in her head.

"Of course I do," she said.

"Fine," he told her. "But no funny business."

Karpus picked up Whiskers and all of them walked through the house and up to the third floor. Greer opened his bedroom window and Karpus carried Whiskers out onto his roof.

After Karpus climbed out, Greer followed. When Chloe came out, Greer wrapped his arms around her, locked her in a bear hug.

"I promise I won't do anything," she said.

Greer wanted to believe her. He wanted to let her body go and close his eyes and he wanted her to be there when he opened them, but he could not take that chance.

He and Chloe watched Karpus say his goodbyes to Whiskers. Karpus brought the cat right up to his face and planted a kiss right on the cat's mouth. He whispered into the cat's ear.

Greer thought Karpus was going to keep talking to the cat for a while, reminiscing about all the good times they'd had, but suddenly Karpus tossed Whiskers up into the air.

"Go!" he yelled. "Fly!"

Whiskers plummeted toward the ground. Greer was certain that the cat was going to splatter on the front sidewalk, but just before he hit the ground, Whiskers spread his wings and swooped upward. It looked strangely natural, Greer thought, like the cat was remembering something that was embedded deep inside him, an instinct from a time long past.

As Karpus jumped up and down, cheering the cat, Chloe began to struggle. She reared back and kicked Greer in the shin with her shoe, tried to push one of her thumbs into his eye socket.

"Stop," he told her.

Chloe continued to buck and writhe. Greer would corral her for a second, but then she would wriggle free. Finally Greer got a good grip on her flailing limbs. Chloe quit struggling and they stood on the roof and watched Whiskers become a tiny speck on the horizon. The cat grew smaller and smaller, until it curled over the edge of the earth and disappeared.

THE DOJO

I stole my yoga teacher Michelle's wallet because she was stupid enough to leave it sticking out of her purse for me to steal and because I think there are hard lessons about the real world besides remembering to inhale and exhale that can be taught inside the dojo or whatever the fuck they call it. Michelle had two hundred dollars and a bus card in her wallet and the next day I rode the bus back to the dojo for free and used her cash to buy an unlimited monthly yoga pass.

"I didn't think you liked coming here," Michelle said to me. "You kept saying you hated it."

The real reason I kept coming back here was because Evelyn, a pretty brunette who I stalked occasionally, came here to decompress from me stalking her. Evelyn had recently changed apartments and phone numbers and the yoga dojo was now my best chance to locate her.

"No way," I told Michelle. "It's the exact opposite. I love coming here."

- - - - - - - -

I'd stolen a pair of light blue panties from Evelyn's dresser and now whenever I went to yoga I carried these panties in my pocket to help me achieve Zen or whatever it was called. Sometimes I pulled them out to wipe the sweat from my forehead. The panties were silky and they didn't do much to sop up perspiration, but I used them anyway. I was waiting for Evelyn to show up and see me wiping my brow with them. I thought she might get a real kick out of that.

After class that night, Michelle was outside, smoking.

"Are you supposed to be doing that?" I asked. "Isn't that against your teachings or something?"

Michelle had extremely long arms. When her hand was at her side it took her forever to get her cigarette up to her mouth.

"I was really off my game tonight," she said. "I totally fucked up the tilted crane."

She flicked her cigarette onto the sidewalk and then immediately lit another one.

"Are you okay?" I asked.

"Really bad week," she said.

The next day Michelle was not at class.

"Where's Michelle?" I asked the sub.

"She called in sick," the woman said.

Since I had her wallet, I knew where Michelle's apartment was. After class, with the last of her money, I bought her a bouquet of tulips.

"How did you know where I lived?" she asked me when she answered the door.

"That's not important," I said, holding out the flowers.

I had given women presents before, but usually they were presents that they did not appreciate. This present, though, something felt different. It was like these flowers had pulled our two worlds into alignment, and now she and I were cosmically even or whatever it is people say when something like this happens.

Michelle wrapped her long arms around my neck and pulled me in tight. "This was so sweet of you," she said.

"Really," I whispered into her pretty ear, "it was nothing."

ALEJANDRA

My new lover said he loved me. I told him I loved him back. We'd met only forty-five minutes before, but we both agreed that we were totally and completely in love.

"I have something to tell you, Francine," my new lover told me as we laid naked on my futon.

"More important than our love?" I asked.

"No," he told me, "but pretty important."

Just before this, I had taken my fingernails and written words on my new lover's back. He was supposed to guess the words I'd written there, but he was not very good at this game. I wrote "enchanted" and he guessed "extradited." I wrote the word "forever," but he guessed "foreskin." He turned toward me now, took my hands in his.

"Listen, Francine," he said, "I am pretty sure I have syphilis. Not positive, but pretty sure."

My new lover was pale. He had freckles and moles spread out all over his body. He was young, much younger than me. There was a tiny shamrock tattoo among all the freckles. I understood what he was trying to do there—you had to search for it like it was a real shamrock, right? I don't know why, maybe it was his laidback attitude, but I got the feeling he was Canadian.

When he said what he said about having syphilis, I laughed. I took my hand and I hit it playfully on his freckled, probably Canadian chest.

"Syphilis?" I said. "That's it? You said it was something important."

My new lover's eyes narrowed. I had not seen him this serious in the entire forty-five minutes I'd known him. I'd only known three sides of him so far—angry/sexy and then playful/sexy and now serious/sexy, but I loved all of them equally and decided I would continue to love whatever other sides I saw.

"Syphilis is no joke," he said. "Syphilis will fuck your shit up."

I laughed at him again. I knew it was horrible to laugh at someone you loved when they were so concerned, but I couldn't help myself. I couldn't help myself because actually, syphilis *was* a joke to me. It was a joke because my life was already fucked up. I was already mostly crazy and when I did not put my contacts into my eyes I could hardly make it from my bedroom to my bathroom without catastrophe. What I mean to say is that I did not care about becoming any crazier or blinder, just as long as I would be these things with my new lover.

As we talked, the buzzer of my apartment began going off, rapid fire, these short and insistent bursts.

"Don't you hear that?" my new lover asked.

"Don't I hear what?" I said.

I first saw my new lover outside the Asian grocery store near my house. He was being yelled at by the grocery store owner, Mr. Yu. My lover held his skateboard under his arm and as Mr. Yu yelled at him, he held up his middle finger and told Yu, in perfect Cantonese, to fuck the fuck off.

"Hey!" I yelled as he hopped on his skateboard. "Hold on!"

I was carrying a bag of groceries that I had purchased at the bodega across the street from my apartment. I had stopped going to Yu's grocery store because Yu had found out I'd lived in China and that I spoke Cantonese. After Yu found this out, he said horrible things about his Indian wife to me. His wife sat right next to him at the counter, doing her word jumble and not knowing what Yu was saying. Yu expected me to laugh with him about how fat and ugly and good for nothing his wife was, but all I wanted to do was buy that good coconut milk beverage that Yu's store carried.

"What now?" my new lover asked.

The street lights had just turned on with their hissing and popping and under this silvery light his blue eyes looked lovely. The anger had not disappeared from them yet and I saw that beneath the surface my lover was a complicated young man whose rage quite possibly would be his downfall.

"I bought way too much food," I told him. "I don't know what I am going to do with all of it."

I had used this line on men before, batting my eyelashes and pretending to be helpless or unable to calculate how much a single woman could eat. It had always worked. My first husband, William, the one who I had moved to China with, was propositioned in this very same way.

"This cutlet is much too big," I'd told William. "There's absolutely no way I can eat it all."

I'd invited William back to my kitchen and after we'd eaten, I'd invited William into my bed. Soon after that, we married and moved to China. Once we were there, though, William had left me for a Chinese woman. I imagined that this woman had shown William a heaping bag of mysterious Chinese groceries with eels and oxtails and that she'd pretended to be helpless and stupid too. It was a vicious cycle, this thing with men and food and desire, one that none of us would ever break no matter how hard we tried.

"Look," I said now, tipping down my bag of groceries to show my new lover the contents. "Without you, all of this goes bad."

My lover looked into the grocery bag. Then he looked me up and down. He looked down the block and then he looked at his watch and then he looked at me again.

"I guess I could eat," he said.

As we laid curled up together on my futon, I realized if we never left my apartment to seek a cure for our syphilis our eyes would get crusted over with pink goo and we would moan and shit everywhere and maybe smear our shit on the walls or on my leather sofa, just me and my new love.

"What if we never went outside ever again?" I asked him. "Wouldn't that be absolutely romantic?"

"Would the buzzer be going off all the time?" he asked. "Because that buzzer is driving me apeshit."

I did not want to bore my lover with the mundane details of my daily life. For instance, why the buzzer of my apartment kept going off. I wanted our love to be a huge love, an all-consuming love that transcended time and space. Every love in my life up until this point had ended with both of us alive and angry and now I wanted something different. I wanted something epic, something where I died intertwined in someone's soiled arms and legs.

The reason the buzzer in my apartment kept going off was that a prostitute named Alejandra had lived here before me. She was a prostitute whose specialty was being choked. One night she had gotten choked a little bit too much and I got a discount on my rent now because men who did not know she was dead kept coming to my apartment and buzzing my buzzer.

"Alejandra," the men said to me when I pressed the intercom button. "Alejandra, is that you?"

Sometimes the men got past my security door by mashing their hands over a block of intercom buttons and someone else in my building, someone old or lonely or crazy, would just buzz them up. Then these men stood in front of my door chanting Alejandra's name.

"Maybe it's an emergency," my lover said to me when the buzzer went off. "Maybe it's a long lost friend. You are cordoning yourself off from a lot of possibilities here."

Cordoning. I liked that word. Up until that point, I'd wondered if my new lover was smart enough to hold my attention over the many months we'd be holed up in my apartment, but this word, *cordoning*, made me breathe easier. He was smart enough! He had used the word *cordoning*!

"It's not any of those things," I told him. "It's just someone messing with me."

My new lover looked annoyed at my explanation, but I put my tongue inside his mouth and then I grabbed onto his hips and pulled him down on the couch on top of me.

"I am probably going to give you syphilis again," he told me.

"Of course you are," I said.

I had not totally lied when I met my new lover; I had purchased too much food. I had recently gone to the bulk store and bought an industrial size jar of pickles and a dozen gallon-sized cans of beef barley soup. I had a bag of pretzels that was roughly the size of a twin bed, a wheel of cheese that I had to cut in half to fit inside my fridge. If we didn't overeat, if we didn't get bored eating the same things over and over, we could stay here for a very long time.

"This is messed up," he said, hoisting up the bag of pretzels. "Who could eat all these?"

"Exactly," I said. "Who could eat all of those before they died, you know? Probably not us, that's for sure."

My lover sat down next to me and he lifted my fingers up to his lips, kissed them slowly, one by one. I closed my eyes. I suppose at this point I should have fantasized that we were somewhere else, like on a tropical island with a long white beach and clear blue water, but what I imagined was him and me just sitting right here on my couch a few months from now when we were a little older and a lot crazier.

The buzzer went off again and he dropped my hands in my lap. "Jesus," he said. "Does that thing ever stop?"

I got up from the couch and went over to the kitchen and poured myself a glass of wine from the huge cardboard box on the counter. I took a drink and my new lover snapped a picture of me with his phone. Then he began to push some buttons.

"I just sent your picture to my friend Alex," he told me. "I wanted to show him what I just got down with."

I stood up and he took a few more pictures of me from different angles. Then he sent those to Alex too. My lover's cell phone rang and he answered it.

"Totally," he told the person on the phone. "A total cougar."

My new lover talked to the person on the phone for a couple of minutes. I started to wave at him to get his attention. Hello, I waved, I am over here, remember me?

"Uh-huh," he said to the person on the phone. "Sure, sure. I'll be there in like twenty minutes."

When he was finished talking, my lover stood up and slipped on his pants. Then he pulled his shirt over his head.

"What are you doing?" I asked. "Are you going somewhere?"

"This was fun," he said lacing up his shoes. "But I've got to go now. I've got business."

He stood in front of me now and I suddenly realized how much taller and skinnier he was than me, thought about how sometimes you forget how much taller and skinnier someone is than you when you mostly know them from being on top of or behind you. He kissed my cheek and then he walked toward the door. I could not imagine him leaving now and so I ran over and pressed my body around his. I had plenty of things that I'd used in the past to make men stay—I'm pregnant and it's yours, I just took a handful of your sleeping pills and I am going to die, I'm pregnant and it's yours *and* I just swallowed a handful of your sleeping pills— but none of those would really work in this situation.

"I thought we were in love," I said.

"We're in love," he said. "You can't question that. But business is business."

"There's all this food," I told him. "There's me."

I dug my fingers into his back, but he still pushed his way toward the door. I slid down his body and grabbed his legs, but he pushed me off. I rolled into my coat rack and he grabbed his skateboard and ran down the hall. I got up and chased after him, but by the time I arrived to the street, he was rolling away.

"Go to the clinic!" he yelled back to me. "Make sure you go and get yourself checked out!"

After my new lover was gone, I went back to my apartment and sat on my couch. I covered myself up with a blanket and opened a huge bag of pretzels. I propped the bag on my stomach and ate handful after handful until my lips burned from the salt.

As I sat there, the buzzer went off again. It would not quit this time. I thought it might be my new lover returning to tell me how sorry he was and how much he had missed me, so I got up to look. Instead there was a man in a grey suit standing in the entryway. He had dark, spiked hair and sunglasses. He held a bouquet of orange flowers in his fist.

"What?" I said, pressing the intercom. "What do you want?"

"Alejandra?" the man said. "Is that you?"

I stared at the man standing in the entryway. I did not feel like there was anything wrong with my blood or my brain at this moment, but I knew that there was something inside me now, something my lover had given me that either had to be cut out or killed off for me to continue on.

"Yes," I told him. "It's me. It's Alejandra."

"Can I come up?" he asked.

The man was wearing leather gloves; he was clenching and unclenching his hands, gripping and re-gripping that bouquet of flowers.

"Hold on one second," I said.

I went around and tidied up my apartment. I closed my blinds and I lit a scented candle. I lowered the lights in my apartment and then I pressed the security button and let him in. I heard him running up the stairs. I propped open my door and then I laid down on my bed. I heard his footsteps coming down the hall.

"I'm here," I called out.

I arched my neck. I took a deep breath. I waited for his hands.

IF YOU LIVED HERE
YOU'D ALREADY BE HOME

There are some things you should not do in the rich town up the mountain from yours and one of those is sticking your dick in their mail slots or dog doors and moving it around and thrusting your hips in and out and sometimes urinating, but sometimes not, depending on how you feel and what kind of rug they have and honestly, whether or not you have to piss, but this, this is precisely what my little brother Carl and I started doing one Saturday morning after our baseball season ended.

"This is how revenge works," I told Carl as we biked the hill to Buena Vista. "It's an eye for an eye. And sometimes it is also urine for an eye."

This was the twenty-second straight year that our town had lost to Buena Vista. This was the twenty-second straight year that Buena Vista had gone to the Under 16 Nationals. It was, we kept reading on a number of billboards taken out by THEIR booster club in OUR town, some sort of North American record.

Our town, Cuffs River, took this year's loss badly, but our coach, Ron Turnbull, took it the worst. After the game, instead of taking the exit ramp to his house, Coach Turnbull drove his pickup right off the Cuffs River Bridge. No skid marks or anything. He just decided that enough was enough and floored it right through the guardrail and into the murky runoff below.

"Turnbull was a man of substance," I told Carl. "He just picked a stupid place to live."

Of anyone in Cuffs River, my brother Carl was hit the hardest by Turnbull's death. I'd heard every one of Turnbull's rah-rah speeches two or three times and was annoyed by the chewed up cigar butt that was permanently housed in the corner of his mouth, but Carl loved him. Turnbull had made Carl our team manager. Turnbull had given Carl rides home in his truck every night after practice. Turnbull always had a huge stash of Carl's favorite food, red licorice, in his duffel bag. Turnbull, Turnbull, Turnbull. Carl was so in love with the man that anytime anyone mentioned his name now, in the dollar store or at the swimming pool, Carl would smack himself in the chest two times with his fist and then furiously point up at the sky.

"Toooornbill!" he'd moan.

By now, no one in town paid Carl much mind. He was just another kid who had to wear a hockey helmet wherever he went. Another kid who threw up whenever he got too excited. He was any one of a number of people in Cuffs River who pointed at the heavens and moaned for a lost loved one.

"I'm responsible," Carl told me as we sat on our couch watching TV. Carl had just gone to the barber and gotten his hair cut like Turnbull's, a crewcut, high and tight. "I'm the one."

I got up and walked over to the refrigerator and grabbed a Coke. I snapped it open, slid back down onto the couch. I passed it over to Carl and he took a drink. Carl wasn't supposed to drink anything carbonated, but we were already breaking some of my mother's rules today, so why not break some more? We'd already finished one bag of fun-size candy bars and were halfway through another.

"You aren't responsible," I told Carl. "It's not your fault."

One thing you learned in Cuffs River early on—Buena Vista would do whatever it took to beat our asses. They flew in these kids from hot dusty countries, doctored up their birth certificates; put their families up in fancy hotels with cable and air for the entire summer. I know it was weird, but whenever I looked at the map of Central America, I couldn't help but imagine this swarm of hungry and talented young men, bats in their hands, sprinting across the border and running toward our town just to smash my dreams.

"So close you could taste it!" Carl yelled out.

Other than moaning about Turnbull this had been Carl's favorite phrase lately. Whenever he said it, he took his fingers and smashed them together until just the tiniest gap remained.

The really sad thing about this year was I thought it was THE YEAR. Of course, I had thought that about the year before too. And the year before that. I guess I thought it every year. I knew Ron Turnbull did too, but this year, man, I think we both really thought it.

During the off-season, while every other kid was screwing off, my team got together and ran the canyon roads. In our algebra class, whenever Mr. Benson turned his back, we worked on our signals. Eric Kowalke, the catcher on our team, set up a makeshift batting cage in his garage and we rode our bikes over there on the weekends and hit off a tee into a drop cloth. This spring, when we ran out onto the field, I thought that this extra work would pay off. I thought that this year Buena Vista would be bitching about *us* playing on ESPN.

"Toornbill," Carl moaned again.

I was sick of taking care of Carl. I was sick of him saying the same things over and over again. I was sick of Buena Vista always beating our asses.

We'd just moved into this new apartment the week before and

there were cardboard boxes surrounding us, stacked up against the walls. I walked over and kicked one of the boxes as hard as I could. It fell into another one, tipped that one over and a couple more tumbled off the pile and onto the floor.

I walked over into the kitchen and grabbed another soda. I looked at Carl. His new haircut wasn't doing much for him. With short hair his head looked like a relief map—raised mountains, lowered valleys, buttes.

"I'm sorry, buddy," I told him after I'd calmed down. "Kicking stuff. I lost it there for a minute. That's not cool."

Even with the volume on the television blaring, I could hear Carl's stomach gurgle. Then he started to gag. I ran to the kitchen and grabbed the garbage can and hurried into the living room, but it was already too late. The contents of Carl's stomach, everything we'd eaten and drunk that afternoon, spilled out in a watery brown pile in the middle of the floor.

My mother was working to try to get us out of Cuffs River. She'd been talking about this for the last two years, but hadn't made much headway. She worked two full-time jobs just to keep us afloat, a day job at a florist and then one at night at a bakery decorating cakes. Every night, she came home around ten. She was dead tired and all she could do was flop down on the couch and beckon me over to rub her feet.

I pleaded with her to take a personal day, but she waved me off.

"I write the thank you's. I pen the love notes. I tell the spouses sorry," she said. "There aren't any days off."

She was swamped at both her jobs—everyone in Cuffs River kept on dying and cheating on each other and having birthdays and anniversaries and she had to put whatever it was they told her onto a tiny card and stuff it into a tiny envelope. Or fit everything on top of a sheet cake.

"Here," I said, shoving a drink box at Carl. This was one of the rules—keep him hydrated. If you didn't, he'd have a seizure where he'd try to bite his tongue off and you'd have to grab his arms and legs and pin him down so he didn't knock a bookcase on top of himself.

I went to get some paper towels to clean up his mess. I listened to him slurp down the drink box, burp loudly, overemphasize an *Ahhhhh*. He moved over and started to open another miniature candy bar, like nothing had happened. I ran over and snatched the bag from him. I put it back into the cabinet, snapped the padlock back on the door. He glared at me, pursed his lips and shook his head, but I pointed over to the pile of puke on the floor.

"You really think that is a good idea?" I asked. "Just tell me you do. Tell me *all* about it, buddy."

I got down on my knees, wiped up what I could with paper towels and then started scrubbing the carpet with a sponge. Sad to say, but I was used to Carl's puke by now. The sour apple smell it gave off hardly even fazed me. I tried not to get angry about it anymore. This was just Carl. He was a force of nature and it was better to just resign yourself to that fact.

The first Saturday we biked up to Buena Vista, I had to convince Carl to come with me.

"Why?" he asked. "These are the dog days of summer. The dog days. Way too hot."

"Turnbull," I told him. For me, this was about other things, but I knew saying Turnbull's name was a call to arms for Carl.

"Tooornbill is gone," he said pointing up at the ceiling in our apartment. "Not coming back."

"If you let him be gone, he's gone," I told Carl. "But," I said pointing at my heart, "he can live here." I knew this was a fucked-up thing to do, to play with Carl's emotions like this, but the truth was that I didn't want to bike up to Buena Vista alone.

Carl sat silent, mulled it over.

"Okay," he said. "Fine. Dog days be damned."

He still looked reluctant when we got on our bikes, so on our way up to Buena Vista I took him past the spot where Turnbull had driven off the bridge. It was on the road just before the turnoff to the paper factory that made our town smell like burnt toast. The city had put up a cement barrier there on the bridge, but they'd never replaced the guard rail. The metal was splintered and gaping, like a mouth stuck open in a scream.

"See?" I said. "No tire rubber. No skid. When you don't skid, it means you want it. It means you want whatever is ahead."

I'll admit, I'd been thinking about Turnbull a lot lately too. Probably not as much as Carl, who thought about him almost every waking moment. At night, when I couldn't sleep, I thought back on all the times that Turnbull had yelled at me to charge a grounder. How he told me that my footwork was shit. How he showed me to drop the end of the bat to deaden a bunt. Who would do that now? Who was going to tell me what I needed to work on? Was I supposed to figure that stuff out by myself?

Plus there were the postcards.

At our team banquet the week before, I found out that before he died Turnbull had mailed postcards to the team. During the banquet, my teammates and I got together in the bathroom and compared them. Carl and I hadn't gotten one, but we looked them over as they got passed around. Turnbull was dead and yet here he was, still dispensing his wisdom. The postcards he'd sent out were these old time black-and-white nudes, girls with shy smiles on their faces and mounds of hair covering their crotches. We read the things Turnbull had written on them out loud. Some of his words were positive—simple stuff like, "Keep your head up, Grundahl." Others were more personal in tone. "Your father is a drunk, Highsmith. The sooner you and your mother ship out of Cuffs River, the better."

In the note he sent our first baseman, Aaron Blasgovich, Turnbull gave pointed advice.

"Get as much pussy as you can before you die," he wrote. "Trust me. On your deathbed you won't think back on your lovely wife. You'll think back on the nasty whores."

Carl and I looked at the postcards, laughed at them along with everyone else, but there was no way not to feel left out.

"What about us?" Carl asked me. "Where's our postcard?"

"Maybe he didn't have our new address," I told him, even though I didn't believe that was the case. "Maybe it got lost in the mail."

Carl pondered that for a second, but then he started choking on a piece of hard candy I'd given him. He was never supposed to get hard candy, but he'd begged and begged. The problem with hard candy was that Carl always lost track of what he was doing and just swallowed it. This time, I'd made him promise that he'd concentrate on what he was doing, but he'd forgotten. Luckily, I was well schooled in the Heimlich by now, so I calmly came up behind him and pulled up on his ribs. The piece of candy flew across the bathroom and landed on the tile. It shattered into a bunch of tiny red shards.

"Maybe you are right," Carl said without missing a beat.

Carl and I wore our baseball uniforms every time we rode up to Buena Vista. We were in full gear, stirrups and baseball pants. We had on the black mesh tops with "Kiko's Heating and Cooling" on the front and our names and numbers screen printed on the back.

On the road there, we rode past the abandoned car factory where my father had worked before he'd split town. He worked there for ten years and then one day he was replaced by a robot welder. Then the robot welder wasn't cheap enough and the whole company moved to Mexico. Now the factory sat empty, rusted barbed wire running along the top of the chain link.

We rode past that recycling place with all the dead computer monitors in a big pile. Past the place that had that tire fire a few years back that turned the sky black for a week.

After about an hour of biking up hills, zigzagging back and forth up the switchback roads, it flattened out. We came upon the town sign. Buena Vista. Population 64,518. We took a turn off the main drag and rode into the residential area.

Most of the time it was hard to keep track of where we were. All of the houses looked the same. They were all huge and painted beige and they all had neatly cut lawns. I don't know how we told these places apart, but it didn't really matter. Maybe I stuck my dick in some of the places with dog doors or mail slots two or three times. Maybe more. Maybe it was twenty. It wasn't like I was keeping track. I was angry and out for revenge. There wasn't any sort of logbook that I kept—I just knelt down by the front door of any house that looked safe and unbuckled my pants and put my dick inside and shook it around. If I had to piss, I pissed.

Was I worried about dogs? Fuck yes. Was I worried about people? Sure. That was why I needed Carl as my lookout.

Even though I knew Carl did not comprehend the significance of this act of revenge, I went on and on about it, about why we were here, why this was necessary.

"We are not going to take the hand we were dealt," I told him. "It is about them having all this and us having shit. Sticking our dicks in these houses is symbolic."

"For Tornbill too," Carl would add. Carl had this exaggerated head nod that sometimes took over his whole body and you had to put your hand on his shoulder to settle him back down.

"Yes, of course, for Turnbull," I said.

The best part of the day had nothing to do with the houses. The best part was riding our bikes back down the hill, knowing what we had accomplished. Revenge is a sweet fruit, and hearing our bikes fly down that huge hill, our spinning wheels whirring loud and constant, it was like a rousing cheer that was always just a little ways off.

One Saturday, about a month after we started to exact our revenge on Buena Vista, I stuck my dick into a house and met someone. Carl was supposed to be watching the door, but he'd gotten tired. He was sitting on the stoop paging through a comic book, not paying attention.

"Someone touched me," I told him. "Tugged on it, then let it go. Then giggled, I think."

"Are you sure?" he asked. "Not the wind again?"

I had made this accusation before. I thought I had felt some other fingers on me at various times in Buena Vista, but hadn't ever been able to get any corroboration.

"This time I know what I felt," I said. "This time it wasn't the wind."

I tucked myself back in, started walking back to my bike and then the door swung open. There stood a girl. She was around my age, with a small nose and her blonde hair up in pigtails. She was wearing a track sweatshirt and some running shorts.

"My father is in his den with some clients," she said. "But I still could go tell him what you just did. I still might."

At that moment all I could think about was my mom's face when she picked us up at the station, how disappointed she'd be. I looked over at Carl. I saw he was thinking about getting ready to puke, his lips smacking together. If I played it cool, like this was not out of the ordinary, I might settle his stomach before something happened.

"If you were going to do it, you would have done it by now," I told the girl.

The girl looked us up and down. It wasn't hard for her to tell where we were from, what was wrong with Carl.

"I guess you're right," she said.

She turned and walked in the house without closing the door. The back of her sweatshirt said "Lily Buns." She began to walk up the stairs and then motioned for us to follow.

"C'mon already if you're coming," she told us.

We tiptoed up the stairs behind her. The air inside her house smelled like lilacs. There were flowers spilling out of vases everywhere you looked. She led us up to her room. There was a small fridge up there sitting by her bedside and she walked over to it and pulled out a couple of Cokes and handed them to us. We sat down on the side of her bed. Carl snapped open his Coke and started slurping it down.

"Slow down," I cautioned.

Carl nodded at me and then his whole body started nodding and I put my hand on him and stopped his nodding. Lily Buns was watching the entire thing.

"Just so you know, my father would kick my ass if he knew you were up here," she said. "He's really strict."

Lily Buns walked over to her closet and got out a belt. Then she took it and hit it on the side of her bookshelf. It made a loud thwacking sound that echoed throughout the room.

"Sometimes my father hits me with this," she told us. "But then he buys me things. I guess it evens out."

Her eyes started to fill with tears, but then she smiled and they slid back inside her head. I wanted to say something, say how bad that sounded, how much that sucked that her dad did that to her, but she just kept on talking, not leaving any room for me to speak. I looked over at Carl again; he'd moved over by the window and was looking through her stack of computer games.

"My mom's dead," she told us. "Car accident. Six months ago. She was fucking my dad's CPA. My parents were probably going to get a divorce anyway. But then she died so they didn't have to. That fucking CPA came to the funeral, made a big scene. He kept on yelling that he deserved to be there too. He ran up and grabbed onto the urn and started moaning and screaming about how unfair life was. My dad walked up and punched him right in the nose. There was this trail of blood that ran right from her urn out into the parking lot where his car was parked."

Lily Buns paced around her room, picking up things on her dresser, twirling them around in her hands. She wouldn't sit still; she kept on touching down on furniture for a second and then bouncing back up like she had been shocked.

"I've heard about you two," she said. "Jamie Cavanaugh's mom complained to my dad about somebody pissing on her rug."

I looked around. Everything was really clean here. Everything was in its place. Her pillows were fluffed and her bed looked comfortable. It was warm and the lights were low. My arms started feeling heavy. I stood up, shook them out, moved over to the window. I knew I shouldn't relax. I knew that this wasn't safe, but it really felt like it was.

"That was us," Carl said to her. "That piss was his."

I moved over by her CD rack and flipped through what was there. Lily Buns walked over near me, whispered in my ear. I saw Carl lean in from where he was standing, straining to hear what she was saying.

"Make your brother go wait outside," she said.

"For what?" I whispered back.

"I want to see it again," she said.

I looked over at Carl. He was still sitting on the edge of the bed now. This wasn't how it was supposed to be. We hadn't planned on any of this. We'd been invited in. Some girl was asking to see my dick. This didn't feel like revenge anymore.

"No," I said. "We've got to get back home."

She turned to Carl.

"Hey you," she said. "You want another Coke?"

Carl nodded, but I answered for him, "He's finished. We're leaving."

She ignored me, kept on talking to Carl.

"If you wait in the bathroom," she told him, "you can have two Cokes." She took a can out of the fridge and walked out into the hall. "One now. And then the other one if you sit quiet while your brother and I talk. Do you understand?"

I didn't know what to do. Carl would probably be fine with his comic book, but then again, who knew what could happen with him? Lily Buns set the Coke down in the bathroom and Carl walked in there and sat down on the floor.

"I'm right in here," I said as she closed the door. "If there's any trouble."

Carl couldn't have cared less about being left alone. He was already chugging that pop, flipping through his comic book.

Lily came back over and sat on her bed.

"So we're alone," she said. One of her feet was moving in a circle. Her chest was arched forward.

I scanned the room as I walked over to her. There was a laptop on her desk. She had this science set that was full of beakers and glass things and what looked to be a Bunsen burner sitting on a table on the other side of the room. It looked like it hadn't been used at all. There were pictures everywhere. One of her in a cheerleading outfit holding pompons up in the air. One of her running in a track meet. Grabbing a baton from another girl.

"Where were we?" she asked.

I didn't have time to answer because she immediately jumped up and pushed me down on her bed. She straddled me and then she pulled her sweatshirt over her head. She was wearing a light blue bra. She moved her lips into mine. I had gotten some action before with a couple of girls in Cuffs River, but nothing close to this. She pulled her mouth away from me.

"Your turn," she said. She pulled my baseball jersey off over my head and then she slid off my shoes. She unbuckled my pants. I turned to look at the door, but she spun me back towards her, pressed up against my chest. She started to kiss me hard, smacking her teeth against mine. That is when I noticed the tears. There was no whimpering, just tears, streaming from her eyes.

"Are you okay?" I asked her.

"This is how it works," she said. She sounded calm; her voice wasn't shaky at all. She pulled off her shorts. She wasn't wearing any panties under them. "This is how it works with me, okay?"

Tears kept coming down her cheeks. She looked sad, but angry too, her mouth was twitching, like she was getting ready to yell. I was hard and she grabbed my dick in her hand. She crouched down and put her mouth near it. I let out a little moan.

"See," she said, "it's okay. It's really no problem."

Soon though, she was openly sobbing, her shoulders heaving up and down. I pushed her away.

"This is weird, right?"

"It's okay," she said to me. "That's just how I am. It's fine. You should just lay back and enjoy it."

I was listening for Carl outside now. I heard him cough. I knew that I needed to get out of here soon. This wasn't going anywhere good.

"This was a mistake," I said. "I'm sorry." I pulled my pants up and started to gather my clothes from around the room.

"No," she said. "Wait, wait. I can do whatever you want. However you want it."

She was naked and she grabbed my arm and she tried to guide me back to bed, but I twisted out of her grasp. I had my pants and shoes on now, but I was holding the rest of my clothes in my arms. I opened the bathroom door and grabbed Carl and ran down the stairs and out the front door.

We ran across the lawn. Carl was lagging behind me a little and when he heard Lily yelling at us, he turned to look at her.

"Go, then!" she yelled. "Go on back home with your retard brother!"

Carl stopped running and turned around and stared at her. She had put her clothes back on and was standing there on her front lawn, yelling at us.

"Pussies!" she screamed. "Broke-ass fucking retard pussies!"

A strange look came over Carl's face. I thought he was going to puke, but instead he ran at her. He was moving in his slow and plodding way and as he ran he let out a low growl. Lily Buns saw him coming and started to laugh.

"Oh great," I heard her say.

When Carl actually got to her, she easily sidestepped him. He ran past her, his momentum carrying him into their front hedge. He fell into it, his legs kicking up in the air.

"Jesus Christ," she said before she walked back inside.

I'd asked Carl a couple times if he was okay as we rode off down the hill, if there was anything he needed, but he just shook his head. He wasn't talking to me. He was staring straight ahead, pedaling his bike, breathing through his mouth. When we got home, he tromped up the stairs and went into our room and shut the door.

On the kitchen table was the day's mail and I saw that our postcards from Turnbull had finally come. They were addressed to our old apartment. They had come with yellow forwarding stickers on them.

"Ricky," mine read, "I am gone now. What does that feel like, you may ask? It doesn't feel any different yet (since I am not totally dead at this moment when I am writing this). Still, it feels strange to be on one side of something and know that you will be entering the other side soon. Can you know? Probably you cannot. You are fifteen years old. You guys never knew shit."

It was signed "Coach Turnbull." I held the postcard in my hands. Read it over again. I looked at the naked girl on the postcard. She looked scared to be there. She looked like the camera had surprised her. She looked like someone had talked her into being there and now she had realized that this was a big mistake.

I went into our bedroom and sat down next to Carl on the bed. I handed him his postcard.

"Here," I said. "It's from Turnbull. It says, 'Carl, be good.'"

Carl sat there for a long time holding his postcard, rotating it from the words to the picture. After a while, he hit his chest two times and pointed to the sky and quietly mouthed Turnbull's name.

I sat with him for a while, watching him, and then I went into the living room and ripped open a moving box on top of the pile.

First I unpacked the silverware and put it into the drawer. Then I unpacked the glasses from their newspaper, washed them and put them into the cabinets. I unloaded a box of books, slid them away onto the bookshelf.

I was flying around the room for the next few hours, throwing things into cabinets and closets. Carl got up and came over to me and asked me if he could help.

"Sure," I told him.

And we worked for a long time, arranging our new place, putting everything on shelves and into drawers. By the time my mother got home that night, there was not much left for her to do.

THE GIRL WITH THE GAMBLING MOTHER

The girl with the gambling mother comes back from Christmas break missing a pinky. Her mother brings her back to school in a conversion van with a picture of Tom Brady spray painted on the side. The gambling mother is a big Patriots fan and we, the staff of Middleton Primary, can only think the worst. That the gambling mother lost. That instead of giving up the van, the gambling mother gave up the girl.

The girl comes back wearing the same hooded Patriots sweatshirt she always wears—heather grey with a chocolate stain that looks like a coiled-up snake. Her hand is wrapped in gauze and over the gauze she wears a thick wool mitten. I thought the other kids would be scared of her, but they are not. Instead of shying away, they crowd around her and ask to see. Show us, they plead, show us what isn't.

"I was cutting bread," the girl tells them as she spins off the gauze, "and the knife slipped. Then my pinky was on the floor and my dog scooped it up and ran outside. We think it's buried somewhere in our backyard, but we aren't totally sure."

Mr. Reylindo, the school's social worker, pulls the girl from gym class every morning to discuss her missing finger. He gives her a sock puppet to act out what happened. She sticks to her story about the bread knife and the golden retriever. She never tells us that it is her mother's fault even though this is the thing we want her to tell us most.

"Sooner or later," Mr. Reylindo tells me. "Sooner or later I always get the truth."

I have a short but checkered history with Mr. Reylindo. We went on a couple of dates last fall. Once we did some poppers and went dancing. One night we smoked some weed and went for sushi. The last time we went on a date, we took acid and drove to the tide pools and his wife found us and hit the hood of my car with a machete over and over until Mr. Reylindo got out and told her I was a whore who meant nothing to him.

These days I only speak with Mr. Reylindo out of professional courtesy. I only talk to him when a student of mine has trouble at home. I am done hoping that one night he and I will get into his car and barrel down the highway at top speed, screaming and pounding our fists on the roof of the car because we are full of boundless joy.

"I've missed you," Mr. Reylindo says as we watch the girl through the two-way glass. "I miss the fun we used to have."

I do not answer Mr. Reylindo. I stand there and press my back teeth together so my mouth will not open. I watch the girl pull the sock puppet over her good hand. I watch her play with the sock puppet like it is actually a sock puppet and not some mouthpiece to say all of the things that her real mouth wouldn't dare to say.

I come back from Christmas break straight out of a fourteen-day rehab at Echo Mountain Ranch. I come back to my first graders with a small laminated card that is salmon-colored and says that I am strong and that I can make positive choices about alcohol, drugs, and men. At points in my life I've wholeheartedly believed this statement, but at points my body has bullied my brain aside. It is nice to finally have these words written down for me, wallet-sized, near.

I come back from Christmas break excited to teach, but no more able than I ever was. When you work with small children it is hard not to feel like when the children fail that their failure is also yours. It is hard not to extrapolate things into the future, to guess at what dumbass decisions these kids will make when they are fifteen, twenty-seven, or fifty-six. You wonder whether all the bad choices they make can be traced directly back to you, back to the life lessons you could not drill into their heads when they were young and pliable.

When I come back to my classroom, I build a new reading area with beanbags and throw pillows. I take a gift card that my mother gave me for Christmas and I purchase glue and construction paper. I bring bags of old clothes from my closet so the children can play dress-up. I have tried to make my room a sanctuary, and while it seems to calm the kids, unfortunately, there is no calming me.

"Perhaps you shouldn't go back to school right away," my sponsor, Jillian, warned. "Maybe you want to take a sabbatical. Or maybe you should wait until you find a job at a different school."

I like Jillian, but she's not the sponsor for me. She's too excited about life's possibilities right now. We meet at a coffee shop once a week before our AA meetings and all she does is show me photos of her and her new man, William Bryant. She only refers to him by both his first and last names. William Bryant this, William Bryant that. It's early love, something that I remember fondly. I love early love, but hate late love. I hate love that has already passed by all the fun parts and is fully formed and found to be lacking.

Outside my classroom window, I see the buses pull into the turnaround by the main entrance. I watch kids run out when the doors of the bus accordion open. I get up and pick up a piece of chalk and write the words "Time Capsule" on the blackboard. I stare at these words on the blackboard for a minute before I add an exclamation point behind them. I add the exclamation point to help energize the children; I add the exclamation point because I want them to understand that our next class project will be an exciting one.

After Christmas break, one of the fathers in my class, Steve Senior, starts asking me out. Steve Senior is a nice man with a thick head of wavy hair and hazel eyes. He brings grocery bags brimming with soup labels in for the class. You collect all the soup labels and the school gets something. I have yet to see what we get. In the end it is probably just more soup in bigger cans.

"We should have coffee," he tells me when he comes to pick up Steve Junior. "Get to know each other better."

Steve Senior is not bad looking, but I am not ready for anything right now. I know that this fact does not matter to Steve Senior, that no matter what I tell him he will keep trying. I've sworn off men before, for months at a time, but they are always unfazed by my rejection and continue to operate like they have not heard the word "no" come from my mouth.

"Maybe we can date after Steve Junior isn't in my class," I tell Steve Senior. "Maybe then."

"I trust you to be fair now," Steve Senior says. "I trust that you wouldn't hold anything against my boy."

Steve Junior is a nice kid. Steve Junior is a kid who knows how to share, someone who will give half of his turkey sandwich to anyone who forgets theirs. It doesn't always work this way, but I've found that usually nice kids have nice parents and that sooner or later bad and bad go hand in hand.

"I might hold something against him," I tell Steve Senior. "Or

I might hold something back from you. It wouldn't be fair to any of us, right?"

"Just think about it," Steve Senior says.

And I do. A lot. I lie in bed and think about how Steve Senior could save me from myself. I think about how if I went out with a guy who wasn't named Bandaid or Jayhole, maybe my luck with men would change. But maybe Steve Senior is just like the others, I think, maybe all these men are exactly the same, sitting in wait until I am at my weakest and only then showing me their fangs.

All the other teachers come back from Christmas break bursting with gossip. So and so did this and so and so did that with so and so's this and that. The teacher's lounge is built with thick walls made of cement block and there's a Coke machine in the corner that buzzes really loud. There is no smoking allowed here, but the other teachers cup cigarettes and hold them out the window, let the wind blow the spent ash from the end. Even though this room gives us protection from outsiders, everyone still speaks in hushed tones. They know they shouldn't be talking about these kids, about their parents, but they always always do.

"Did you hear about Greg Kittelson's mother?" the Spanish teacher, Marge Greenwaldt, asks. "Her husband died and she married that butcher at the SaveRite. They shipped Greg off to Arizona to live with his grandparents for a while so they could fuck like bunnies."

Some days my new meds make my skin feel fuzzy like a peach. They make me feel like I can feel each individual hair growing out from each individual pore at an achingly slow rate. I know that if I get started talking about this I will readily admit it to everyone, so I keep my mouth shut unless I am addressed directly.

"What did you do over break?" Jeanne Simoneau, the school's gifted and talented teacher, asks me.

"I went home to visit my mom," I say.

"Where's home?" Jackie Penn, the school nurse asks.

Jackie Penn loves penguins. She has her desk filled with them. Penguin coffee cups, penguin curios, penguin pens. I attempted to make nice with her at the beginning of the school year, brought her this notebook I found at Staples that had a bunch of penguins sliding into a hole on a patch of ice. It got me in her good graces for a while, but then one day I wore a t-shirt that had a polar bear on it. She informed me that polar bears are the natural enemy of the penguins. Now we rarely speak.

"Champaign, Illinois," I say. "I just ate and ate."

Maybe these women could become my confidantes. Maybe they could help me through dark times, help me make positive and fulfilling choices. Perhaps we could drink coffee together and laugh and laugh.

Jeanne Simoneau lights another cigarette and then blows the smoke at me. It hovers around my head. She has never said anything specific about Mr. Reylindo and me, but there is enough disapproval behind her words to make me think she knows what happened.

"Sounds like fun," she sneers.

The gambling mother comes to teacher conferences. She is wearing huge diamond earrings, but I can see that under her makeup, she's got an eye that is far from healed.

"How does this whole thing work?" she asks me.

The gambling mother is wearing a Patriots World Champion t-shirt and a pair of jeans so tight they make my teeth hurt.

"You sit here and I tell you how great your kid is," I say.

While I speak with her, I try not to sound judgmental or mean. I try to give her the benefit of the doubt. I try to put myself in her shoes even though the heels she has on are so high that if I took one step in them I would immediately topple over.

"That's it?" she says. "That's all?"

The gambling mother sits down and I tell her about her wonderful, sensitive daughter. I show her where the girl sits. I open the girl's desk and we look inside. Everything is neat and sectioned off, the pencils lined up along one side, markers in one corner, a notebook laid right in the middle of it all. I guide her mother to the art wall to show her the self portrait that her child has made from kidney, navy, and lima beans.

"She did this?" the gambling mother asks.

"She did," I say. "Your very own daughter."

The gambling mother walks around my room looking at all the pictures. I talk to another parent, Tina Koenig's mother, but I am still looking at the gambling mother out of the corner of my eye. I do not say anything to her when I see one of her diamond earrings fall out of her ear and roll underneath my desk. She does not notice that the earring has fallen. When I am done talking to Sarah's mom, I scoop the earring off the carpet and slide it into my pocket.

"Has anyone seen my earring?" the gambling mother asks.

"Has anyone seen an earring?" I yell out to the room. "Everyone stop moving and look around where they are standing and see if they see an earring on the floor."

Soon all of us are down on our hands and knees scouring the floor. I could stop this, but I do not.

Later that night, Steve Senior comes into my room and I tell him how Steve Junior is doing. They look so much alike, Senior and Junior, and lately when I am in class I look at Junior and wonder what would happen if his father and I were in love.

"Do you want to go for a drink after this is done?" Steve Senior asks. "You probably could use one, huh?"

"Not a good idea," I tell him.

"Why not?" he asks.

I lie to him. I tell him I need to begin work on our time capsule. I tell him that this is very important to the children right now. I tell him that this project will document who we are and what we did during this year. I tell him that this time capsule will be something that tells future people what was important to us in this particular part of the world at this particular time.

"Not even just one drink?" he says.

"I can't disappoint the children," I say.

For the next few days, I find myself sighing more than before, bigger breaths than I ever thought were possible, expanding my lungs to their full potential. At recess now, I see more dust than air. I watch it float by, cut by the sun, and I wonder what it is that I am really opening my lungs up for. One of the ladies in the principal's office, Alexis, wears a portable hepa-filter and while everyone disparages her in public, in private we bombard her with questions.

"Where did you get it?" I ask. And then, "Will it save my life?"

The girl with the gambling mother still seems unburdened. When we mold clay in art class, I wait for her to build something dire and menacing, something that is a testament to a missing finger. I wait for her to build something that means her mother has betrayed her, put a price on her time on this earth. I want the girl to build something like this, but she does not.

"Is it a bean?" I ask her when she shows me the clay she's molded. "Is it a box?"

She waits a minute, takes a long look at me. The artist-in-residence who comes to the school has told me not to guess at the children's work anymore. The artist-in-residence wants me to ask the children other questions, more open and less leading, questions like, "What would that be used for? Would it be something you could eat? Could it fly or does it walk?" I always forget these things. I get too excited—I want to tell the children what they have made. I want to name it for them.

"It's a duck," the girl says. "It's just a duck."

Today when the children are at lunch, I take her mother's earring out of my desk. I slip it into the hole in my ear. I go into the bathroom and stare at myself in the mirror. "Am I still youngish looking?" I ask myself. "How many decent years do I have left?"

One night after school, instead of going home, I follow the girl with the gambling mother's bus. She gets off the bus and skips up the front stairs of her house. She takes a key from under a flowerpot and opens the front door. I get out of my car and crouch in the bushes in front of her dining room window. I watch her move around inside her house. I stand in front of the window and press my face up against it. The glass fogs up but I wipe it away. I see the girl take a bag of chips from a cabinet and then sit down in front of the television. I stand there in the bushes for the next few hours, just watching. Finally she nods off, her face basking in the blue light of the TV.

I follow her home the next night and the night after that too. On the third night, after she falls asleep, I take the key from under the flowerpot and I let myself inside.

The house smells like cigarettes and maple syrup. A pile of empty dishes are sitting in the sink. I stand over her and listen to her short and insistent breaths. I stare at her flawless skin. I feel my heart filling itself with immediacy and dread, but I move closer to her. I crouch down next to her and I slide my arms underneath her body and lift her up off the couch. I carry her upstairs to bed.

"Mom?" she moans.

"Shhhhh," I say.

- - - - - - - -

I could stop but I do not. I start going over there most nights, sometimes even on weekends. After I tuck her into bed, I sit in my car and listen to the oldies station and wait for her mother to arrive. It's always after midnight when that van of hers pulls up, when she gets out of it and stumbles inside.

Since I am up late almost every night now, I turn short-tempered and impatient. Everyone pays the price. Jillian pays the price because I do not want to suffer her never-ending chatter about her upcoming nuptials to William Bryant. She brings the mock-ups of her invites to the coffee shop, wants me to help her choose a wedding cake. She asks my opinion on whether or not she can pull off a dress with an empire waist.

I am distracted. I stare out the window of the coffee shop at two high school kids standing on the corner selling candy bars.

"What's going on with you?" Jillian asks.

"I haven't been sleeping," I tell her.

"That's it?" she says. "That's all?"

For a second, I think about telling Jillian about the girl, but if I do I know that Jillian will make me stop. Either she'll talk me out of it or she will call someone in who will show me the error of my ways. I do not want that yet.

"That's all," I tell her.

"Nothing else?" she asks. "No urges? No backsliding?"

"Nope," I say. "Nothing like that at all."

The kids pay the price because my patience has grown thin. We are horribly behind on the time capsule now. I can't find the right words to help them understand why we are doing this.

"I need you to imagine one hundred years from now," I explain. "I need you to picture someone cracking open the capsule. What would be interesting for these future people to see inside?"

The kids look at me vacantly. One child, Peter Cedeno, holds up a pencil.

"Would a pencil be something interesting to them?" he asks.

Another child, Eloise Randle, holds up a pair of scissors.

"What about these?" she asks.

Jacob Moscovitz raises his hand.

"Can we put my cat Moses inside it?" he asks.

I shake my head no.

"Think of it like a present for people who are not born yet," I tell my class. "Like a present for your children's children. Or their children's children."

The kids still don't understand. Alex Tambola asks if he can put Greta Houser's doll in the time capsule so that Greta will cry. Greta asks if she can stuff Alex Tambola inside so that Alex will die choking for air.

One night as I sit outside the girl's house waiting to go inside and carry her off to bed, Steve Senior taps lightly on the passenger window of my car. He gives me a little wave. I roll down the window.

"I've been stalking you for the last couple of days," he says. "Just so you know."

I unlock the door and let him in. I imagine this is the point where he will start blackmailing me. He won't call it that though. He'll call it an agreement. He will probably get mad whenever I refer to it as blackmail.

"I think I understand what's going on here," he says.

"What do you think you understand?" I snap.

A delivery truck drives by us, its headlights tracking slowly across both of our faces like they are being scanned or copied. The lights slide away and I realize how short the days are getting now, how the days are mostly darkness now.

"It's not your job," he says.

"Then whose fucking job is it?" I ask.

"I don't know whose, but I know it's not yours," he says.

Steve Senior's face is close to mine. I notice he has a small band of freckles that stretches across the bridge of his nose. I hadn't noticed them before. I can't tell if they are new or if they are fading away, if they are something that is disappearing because he is aging or if they are age spots, something that will grow darker over time.

"You are going to lose everything," he says. "You understand that, right?"

I look inside the girl's house now. The light in the living room is still on. It's started to drizzle and from here the light stretches out across the lawn like a beacon on a far away shore.

"You're going to stop?" Steve Senior asks me. "Now that I caught you, you're going to stop, right?"

The class is coming in from recess now, red faced from the spring wind. We are going to start filling our time capsule today. The children have brought things from home. I know I will need to explain it to them again. I will have to tell them about how we will dig a deep hole. I will tell them about how we will put everything inside the metal capsule and then how we will drop the capsule into the earth.

They will still not understand. This much I know. They will stare at me and wonder what good this will do them. They will squirm in their chairs and whisper about me when my back is turned. What is that stupid lady talking about? they will ask each other.

I will tell them that when the time capsule is unearthed and popped open what we've put inside it will be scrutinized to death. All of us will need to live with our choices, with what we've put inside. We'll need to be careful, I'll tell them, because not a single damn one of us will be around to explain any of it.

ACKNOWLEDGMENTS

First and foremost, this book would not exist without my wife Kate Condon, my parents Greg Jodzio and Cilla Diethelm, and my sister Clare Jodzio-McDermott. Unconditional love is a great thing. A large and boisterous cheer to all of the Jodzios, McDermotts, Streckers, Condons and Diethelms for their unflagging support throughout these many years. To my boys, Adam Johnson and Neil Vachhani—each one of those spots on my liver was absolutely worth it. My eternal gratitude to the McKnight Foundation, The Jerome Foundation, The Anderson Center, The Loft Literary Center, the Minnesota State Arts Board, and L'Associazione Culturale Torri Superiore for providing me valuable time and solace. Please raise a glass to Baker Lawley and Robert Voedisch, who saw many of these stories in their infancy and knew exactly what needed to be done. Lastly, a huge debt is owed to Bernard Cooper, Hannah Tinti, and to my lovely aunt, Susan Strecker Richard, who have helped me in innumerable writerly ways that I doubt I can ever repay.

ABOUT THE AUTHOR

John Jodzio's is a winner of the Loft-McKnight Fellowship and the author of the story collections *Get In If You Want to Live* and *Knockout*. His work has been featured in a variety of places including *This American Life, McSweeney's,* and *One Story.* He lives in Minneapolis.

Printed in the United States
by Baker & Taylor Publisher Services